DEFINITELY YES

BOOK ONE IN DEFINITELY SERIES

ELLA MILES

Join Ella's Bellas FB group for giveaways and a **FREE** copy
of **Pretend I'm Yours**→Join Ella's Bellas Here

MAYBE, DEFINITELY SERIES

The Definitely Series is a spinoff series of my Maybe Series. While the Definitely Series can be read without having read the Maybe series, it is best read after the Maybe series.

MAYBE, DEFINITELY SERIES:

Maybe Yes
Maybe Never
Maybe Always

Definitely Yes
Definitely No
Definitely Forever

1

SCARLETT

Why are there no hot men in this bar? I sigh. *Why are there no hot men at any bar—ever?*

I take a sip of my gin and tonic as I scour the room, looking for anyone who will do for tonight. This bar used to be the best bar in New York City to pick someone up for a one-night stand. Now, it is just another bar to add to my list of has-beens.

It's a shame really. This bar has everything. It's clean; it has a live band every night, not just on the weekends; and the bartenders here know my drink order without me having to order. It used to be full of life, full of energy, but now, it is nothing more than an overpriced bar with crappy music and no hot men.

As I glance around the large bar, I don't count more than six other people in the bar, only two of which are men. One is too old—my best guess, mid-forties—and the other, I doubt he's eighteen.

"It just ain't what it used to be, is it?" Todd says.

"No, it isn't. I hate to say this, but I'm going to have to find a new bar," I say.

Todd wipes off the counter in front of me. "I hate to say this, but me, too. The tips aren't what they used to be. And if my favorite tipper leaves me—"

"Your only tipper and most attractive customer," I say, smiling.

Todd flashes me his smile that is missing one front tooth. "Only tipper. I won't be able to survive on the measly salary this place pays me. I guess it is off to find greener pastures."

"Yeah, I guess." I frown as I finish off the last of my gin and tonic.

Todd immediately places another glass in front of me, making me smile.

"Thanks, Todd."

"You bet, Scar," he says.

I take the full glass and raise it to my lips, sipping the perfect, cold liquid that I find myself needing more and more after a long day of work. I love what I do, but running Beautifully Bell Enterprises, the fashion and beauty company I own, is exhausting by the end of the day. I need something cold to relax me and a hot man in my bed to reenergize me for the next morning.

As much as I love spending my evening talking with Todd, it's not enough. I need more. I need thrills and excitement to invigorate me. To make me excited to wake up the next morning. I used to have that every night when I was twenty-five and a model. I always knew the hippest bars to find an attractive man. Half of the time, I didn't even have to go to a bar to find a man. The male models I worked with that day would more than do.

Now, at thirty-two, I've found that it is harder to find a good man for one night. I don't model as much anymore. I just don't have time with my fashion empire. And then men my age are beginning to become more and more interested in more than just one night. They want marriage and babies and the whole package. I'm just not ready for that yet.

That leaves me with the twenty-something-year-old men who are practically still babies themselves. Men who are excited about the idea of one night only. Men who don't care that I'm older than them. Men who like being controlled by a more domineering woman.

My phone buzzes against the table, and I turn it over to see who messaged me.

Kinsley: Emergency! Can I meet you tomorrow? Have news!

My heart races when I see the words *Kinsley* and *emergency* in the same line.

My best friend has been through too much in the past. It's been almost ten years now since she found out her family was money launderers, smugglers, and killers. Ten years since my best friend almost died at the hand of her own grandfather. Now, she's living her happily ever after here, in New York City.

But seeing her text message has me worried that something has happened again. It's after midnight, and my best friend is never awake this late on a Thursday.

I type frantically.

Me: Where are you? Do I need to call the police? What's happening?

I stare at my phone, gripping it much too hard, as I wait for the message to get sent and read.

Come on, come on, I think as I frantically bounce my legs up and down, hoping that she will respond quickly. *I should have just called her, but what if she is stuck in the back of a trunk somewhere? Then, if I called her, it would let her kidnappers know that she had a phone? What if her mouth is taped shut with duct tape, and she can't speak? What if—*

Then, I watch as three dots appear on the screen, indicating that she is typing a response. My phone buzzes in my hand as the message comes through.

Kinsley: LOL. Sorry, didn't mean to scare you. There is nothing wrong. I'm completely fine. Just have some happy news that I can't wait to tell you tomorrow! We've been having trouble with finding time for each other lately, so I just wanted to make sure you knew that I really need you to drop everything and just be my best friend tomorrow.

I shake my head at my friend.

Me: Chica, you just about gave me a heart attack, and then you wouldn't have been able to share your news with me. Just name the time and place, and I'll be there tomorrow.

Kinsley: Eileen's Cheesecake. 1:30 p.m.?

I laugh at her message. *Since when does my friend think it is a good idea to skip lunch and just go straight for dessert? Sounds like I am finally rubbing off on her.*

Me: Done.

I smile, excited to take a break tomorrow to go be with my best friend. It has been a while since I have seen her. *Three months? Or is it four?*

Even though we live in the same city, we might as well live on different continents. With my busy schedule, it's too hard to find time to see each other. Especially since Killian, her husband, doesn't like the idea of us going out to pick up guys for me at night. I need to change that.

I pull up my calendar on my phone. *Shit.* I have meetings all afternoon. *Not anymore,* I think, smiling. I hit Delete on every single one that starts after one o'clock and then type in *Afternoon with Bestie,* starting at one thirty p.m. instead.

I open my email and type a quick message to my assistant, Preston, to cancel everything and reschedule for later. I also tell him to make sure I have an hour or two in the afternoon at least once a week to make time for my friends. I've worked hard enough these last ten years. I think I deserve an hour or two break to actually enjoy the money I make and spend time with my friends.

I should also think of planning a vacation soon. Maybe see if Kinsley and Killian would want to tag along. I'm sure I could find plenty of men to enjoy my time with if we went to a beach in the Caribbean or Mexico. So, I tell Preston to find a good time in my schedule to do that, too. I hit Send, knowing that Preston is going to hate me when I come into the office tomorrow, but he can handle it. It's my business, and if I decide I need a break, then I need a break.

I feel better already as I take another sip of my gin and tonic. I might not be going home with a man tonight, but at least I can go home, feeling good from the alcohol and knowing that tomorrow is going to be a good day.

I finish my fourth drink.

"Another?" Todd asks although he knows I usually stop after four, my usual limit for feeling good without over-doing it.

"A shot of tequila and then another gin and tonic."

Todd raises his eyebrows at me, but doesn't question me as he goes about making my drinks. "What's got you in a better mood?"

"My best friend has good news that she is sharing with me tomorrow."

"I thought I was your best friend," Todd says, placing the shot and glass of gin and tonic in front of me.

"Best guy friend." I wink at him. I raise the shot glass. "To my best guy friend."

Todd smiles, and to my surprise, he raises his own shot glass. We clink the glasses together and then both down our shots. The tequila burns in the best possible way as it goes down my throat.

My phone buzzes again, and I expect to see a message from Kinsley. Maybe she wants to meet up tonight after all. I doubt she will be able to keep her good news to herself any longer. But it's not from Kinsley. In fact, I have no idea who it is from. I open the text message.

Unknown: I want you, just for tonight. I want to make you feel things you have never felt before. I've been watching you all night, Beauty. You're exactly what I want.

I stare down at my phone, confused as to what is going on. I glance over at Todd, assuming it is a prank, but he is deep in conversation with the older gentleman who is now sitting at the bar instead of at one of the pub tables.

Hmm...

Me: I think you have the wrong number.

My phone buzzes again almost immediately.

Unknown: I have the right number, Beauty. I want to shred into pieces that little red dress you're wearing that hugs your overwhelming curves. I want to tame that mane of long, wavy brown hair. I want to feel your tan legs wrapped around my waist until you dig your black pumps into my back so hard that I have to punish you for the pain you have caused me.

I bite my lip as I stare at the seductive message I just received. A message that seems like it is meant for me. The woman he is describing fits me to a T. I uneasily shift in my seat at the thought of having a stranger stalking me. Someone has been watching me, but I can't deny that the thought of a sexy man trying to seduce me via a text message turns me on. It does—more than I would ever admit to this stranger.

I pick up my gin and tonic and spin in the barstool until my back is to the bar, trying to act as casual as possible as I scan the room. But I don't see anyone new who could be sending this. I sigh. *And how would a stranger get my number anyway?*

Todd.

I turn back around and wait impatiently for Todd to find his way back down the bar to me.

"Did you give my number to any strange men?"

"Nope. Why would I want to give any other man a chance to snag my girl?" He smiles.

I wonder if Todd really thinks that way or if it's just a joke in the same way we tease each other about our choice of TV shows. Todd isn't bad-looking. The only odd thing about him is his missing tooth that he told me he'd lost when playing ice hockey. To some women, that would even be a turn-on. He's about my age, but he's just not my type. Not dangerous enough. And I see him more as a friend than a lover.

I look back at my phone. *If Todd didn't give this person my number, then who did?*

Me: Who is this? Who gave you my number?

Unknown: It doesn't matter who I am. All that matters is, we both want the same thing. One night of danger, passion, and mystery. One night that will forever be burned in your memory. One night that will ruin you, so every time you fuck another man, you will think about tonight and wish he were me. Wish he could thrill you the same way that I could.

I read his message, and it's like he has been reading my thoughts. It's exactly what I want. It's what I *need*. But I still don't know exactly what he is proposing. I begin typing to ask him that very question, but I receive his message first.

Unknown: Will you meet me in my room on the top floor of the Waldorf, Beauty? I want to fuck you until you're so sore that you can't walk without thinking about me tomorrow.

My eyes widen as I read his text. I'm supposed to go to a hotel room without even knowing who he is. He could be planning on raping me. He could kill me.

Or he could give me the best night of my life.

I begin to type, *No*, but then stop. *Why am I even considering this? This is crazy! I can't go.*

Kinsley would kill me if she found out. I wouldn't have to tell her though. It would just be one night, and then I would never see this man again. Whoever he is.

He picked the Waldorf, one of the nicest hotels in New York City. He has money.

What if he is that old man sitting down the bar from me? I glance over at him. I study his jeans and button-down shirt. There is nothing fancy or designer about his clothes. His watch is a knockoff. And he's drinking cheap whiskey. He couldn't afford a hotel room like that.

I could ask Todd to go with me. Check out this man and let me know if he's okay first. But that would take all the excitement out of it.

I reach into my purse, making sure the pepper spray I bought after Kinsley had gone missing is still there. It would be my only defense.

I do a lot of kickboxing to stay in shape. I've taken some self-defense classes. Being a single woman, living in New York City, I felt I needed some level of protection. But I know my skills would be no match for a man who is prepared to rape or murder. If he has a gun, I'm fucked. If he surprises me, I'm fucked. If there is more than one man, I don't stand a chance. It doesn't matter how many classes or how strong I am for a woman; most men are still stronger than me. I shouldn't even be considering it.

I hear the door open, and warm, humid air fills the room. I turn just in time to see a tall, dark man leaving. A man in a suit with tousled hair on top of his head. He looks like any typical businessman my age who works in New York. But there is one thing not typical about him. He turns to look at me just before the door closes, and for a split second, I see the danger lurking in his eyes as he stares at me like no man ever has. A danger that pulls at my heart.

I glance back down at my phone and hit the Delete button until I erase, *No*. And then I type, *Yes*, and send the text.

2
___

SCARLETT

FUCK, what am I doing? I walk back and forth in the hallway on the top floor of the Waldorf. I pace in front of the hotel room he texted me after I said yes.

My heart is beating loudly in my chest and races even faster each time I take a step closer to the door and then slows as I walk past it again. Everything in my body is screaming that I shouldn't do this. If I do this, it could be the last thing I ever do. But, somewhere underneath all of that, my body is screaming to knock on the door. To go get the fuck of my life. That, after building a business from the ground up, I deserve this. That I deserve to live a little on the dangerous side.

And, I already said yes. I'm here. I know I won't be able to leave now without knocking on the door. My curiosity, if nothing else, is what is going to get me killed. But at least I'll die without regrets, knowing that I lived my life on the edge instead of in fear and pushed myself to my limits.

I stop in front of the door and knock loudly three times, showing the man on the other side of the door that I'm a confident, strong woman whom he shouldn't mess with.

Not a weak, meek woman who is just doing this because she has no other options.

I wait, but the door doesn't open. Instead, I feel my phone buzz in my pocket.

Unknown: Open the door.

I put my hand on the handle and turn, not expecting it to actually open. It's a hotel room. I don't have a key. It shouldn't open. But it does. I push the door open, hoping to see my stranger. Instead, all I see is darkness.

I step inside, feeling for the light switch on the wall. I find it just as the door swings shut behind me, latching loudly, causing me to jump. As the darkness surrounds me, I flip the switch, but the lights don't turn on. Panic engulfs me as I continue to flip the switch up and down, but no light comes on. I blink rapidly, trying to see past the darkness, but I can't. My hands are clammy as I dig in my purse to pull out my phone for light when I hear his voice.

"Stop."

I freeze. *How can he see me? How can he see what I'm doing when all I see is darkness?*

He must be in the room though, not more than a couple of feet away from me. His voice sounded close. His eyes have probably had time to adjust, while my eyes can't see past the darkness.

I don't know why I listen to him. I don't *take* orders from men. I *give* the orders. I pick up the guys; the guys don't pick me up. I'm my own boss. Men don't control me.

But, for some reason, this man's voice makes me stop. It was so deep and commanding that it makes me want to do whatever he says because behind the voice is a promise that, if I do listen, I will get everything I've ever wanted and more.

But his voice is not enough to keep my own voice at bay.

"Who are you?"

"A man," he answers.

"What's your name?" I try again.

"It doesn't matter."

"Have I met you before?"

"No."

"Do you know who I am?"

"Yes."

I gasp. He knows who I am.

"I don't think it's really fair that you know who I am, but I don't know who you are. I can't even see you," I say.

"It's not, but if I tell you or show you who I am, it will ruin this," he says.

This time, I feel his breath on my neck, causing me to shiver. He's not the man I saw leaving the bar. He's probably hideous or old. That's why he's hiding in the darkness.

"What do you want?"

He laughs, and the deep sound sends more shivers running through my body.

"I thought I made that perfectly clear. You."

"Then, what are you waiting for?"

He chuckles again. "I chose wisely, Beauty. But I need to hear you say it first. I don't fuck women unless they tell me to first."

I don't hesitate. I just say, "Fuck me."

A moment passes as I breathe slowly in and out, waiting for him to make his move. I would make the first move, except I can't see him. And I kind of like the idea of giving up control to a man, not knowing what is coming next, just for one night.

I only get one breath in before my hands are pulled roughly up. Rope narrows around them, binding them together. It's tight enough that I know there is no way I'm ever getting out. He quickly pulls me forward from the hallway and into the next room. I don't know what room this is. I can't make out anything in here either. All I can feel is my arms being jerked rapidly up over my head.

I pull on the rope that must now be tied to something above me because it doesn't give at all. I panic slightly. I've never been one for pain. I've never been one for BDSM. I like my sex full of pleasure without pain, but it seems my stranger is into kinkier things.

I should tell him to stop. That I can't do this. That I need to back out.

"Relax, Beauty. I'm not going to hurt you," he says. "Seeing you in pain isn't what gets me off."

I close my eyes and then slowly open them, trying to push the fear out of my body. Trying to trust this complete stranger. I push most of it away, but there is still a little bit of fear left. Just enough that it amplifies the excitement and anticipation.

"I need you to listen to me, Beauty. I need you to do exactly what I say, and you won't get hurt."

I listen carefully to his words. Each word is dripping with lust and need. Each deep word makes my panties wetter and my nipples harden. Each word makes me think I might have made the right decision.

"Answer me, Beauty. Will you do exactly what I say?"

"Yes," I answer as my voice cracks.

"Good girl."

I feel his body heat as he moves up behind me, but doesn't touch me. He takes his time with studying me, just building the anticipation, before he touches me again until I want to beg him to touch me. I don't. Instead, I wait to see what he is going to do.

Too much time passes. I bite my bottom lip as I wait, but

it does nothing to calm my beating heart. I want him. I've never wanted another man so badly in my life. I want this stranger that already has my heart beating too fast and my stomach in knots.

Finally, I feel his hand sweep my hair off my neck, and his lips land on the back of my neck, kissing me softer than I was expecting, showing me that he isn't going to hurt me. My mouth falls open as I breathe heavily, trying to keep my composure but knowing that it isn't going to last. Soon, this stranger is going to turn me into a sex-needing goddess who can't control herself.

"This dress, Beauty, fits you perfectly, but I'd rather see it on the floor," he says.

His hands drop my hair and then travel over the thin straps of my dress, stopping just above my swollen breasts. My nipples harden, begging him to give them attention, just beneath the thin material. His hands capture my breasts, pushing them together, and I let out a gasp at his sudden touch.

His hands grab my dress in the center and then pull hard, ripping the dress in half, down the front. The thin straps that were holding it on my body come undone. I feel the dress fall to my feet, and then I'm standing, naked, in front of a complete stranger.

I've never been insecure about my body. In fact, I've modeled nude for several magazines before. I love how my body looks. Voluptuous but strong at the same time. Sexy. I've been naked in front of strangers before, but being naked in front of a man I've never seen, one I'm giving up complete control to, this is different. I've never felt this exposed before in my life.

I bite my lip, again, as I wait for him. I feel his eyes going over every inch of my body even though I can't see him.

"You're sexier than I realized, Beauty."

"I know. I want to see how sexy you are, too."

"You don't get to see how sexy I am. You just get to experience it."

"But—"

And then his lips are on mine, shutting me up.

He's right. I can feel how sexy he is from how he kisses. The way his tongue moves around my mouth, massaging my tongue, before his mouth sucks on my lips, drawing me into him. I can feel the stubble from his upper lip brush against my lip, as he pushes his tongue into me further. It makes me think back to the few images I have of the stranger leaving the bar.

It has to be him. He has to be that stranger.

I let the image of that stranger mix with the clues this stranger is giving me of what he looks like. He's tall; I know that much from how he is kissing me in a downward motion, making him taller than I am, even with my heels still on. He's confident and aggressive, yet gentle.

As he kisses me, he gathers my hair into a ponytail on the back of my head and pulls firmly, forcing my head upward, giving him a better angle to kiss me. His body presses against my naked body. He's still dressed. I feel buttons on my breasts, a belt, and a cock pushing against my belly, hidden behind fabric that feels like dress pants.

I pull against the rope, wanting to tangle my hands in his hair, as he kisses me. I want to explore his hard muscles with my hands that I feel against my body. This man works out because all I can feel is hard muscle pushing against me. I can sense his strength in the way he pulls my hair. And I want to feel him. But, no matter how hard I pull against the rope, my hands don't move. They stay high above my head.

When he stops kissing me, I say, "I want—"

"I didn't give you permission to talk, Beauty. No talking. Just feel."

I sigh. I want to talk, to tell him what I want even if he is more than meeting my needs. I'm used to being able to tell a man what to do and how to do it.

I try to be quiet as his mouth returns to mine. It's easy at first as I lose myself in the kiss and as his hand travels over my breast, making me crazy with need, to the point that I forget I'm supposed to be quiet.

"Jesus Christ...I..."

Something hard and round is being shoved into my mouth and then is fastened around the back of my head.

"No more talking, Beauty."

I swallow, trying to get used to the ball gag that is now in my mouth.

He took away the last thing I had control over—my voice. Now, I have nothing left. I can't control my own movements. I can't control what he does to me. I can't control my voice. I've given up all control to this stranger. Everything of me is now his.

I don't know what he is going to do next. I thought my eyes would adjust to the darkness by now, but they haven't. My ears, on the other hand, seem to have gained super-hearing powers now that all my other senses have been dampened. I hear him walking behind me. I hear the rustle of his shirt as he takes it off, exposing what I can only imagine are devastating muscles that I'm dying to see. I hear the loosening of a belt, followed by the drop of his pants.

I suck in a breath, waiting to feel his cock at my entrance. Waiting to feel his hands on my breasts. Waiting to lose myself in him.

Time passes slowly as I wait, and I know he is doing it

on purpose. The longer he waits, the crazier I become, the more I don't care that he is a complete stranger. I don't even know his name or what he looks like or what his intentions are. All of those thoughts drift out of my mind until the only thing I care about is him fucking me.

By the time he speaks to me, I've already become completely lost. Lost in the adrenaline firing through my body—a feeling that, no matter how many men I've had, has never felt like this. He wouldn't even have to touch me again, and I would still consider this one of the top sexual experiences I have ever had.

"Spread your legs," he says, his voice commanding.

I spread my legs apart without hesitation.

It doesn't make sense at all, but I've never felt stronger than while standing here, naked, in front of this man who keeps calling me Beauty. I've never felt more empowered even though I don't have any control. I have all the control because, without me saying yes, this would have never happened. And he knows that, at any second, I could turn that yes into a no.

"Good girl."

He's quiet for a moment. And I don't feel him touching me. I have no idea what he's doing, but the waiting is making me mad. I pull against the rope again, but it remains firmly against my skin. I can't do anything but try to slow my breathing and wait and imagine what he is going to do to me, how his cock is going to feel inside me.

"So wet, Beauty," he finally says.

His words make me pant around the ball gag because that is about all I can do in this position.

My eyes narrow, trying to search for his that I know must be locked somewhere between my thighs where moisture has been gathering quickly ever since he stripped me bare. I'm surprised when his hand doesn't immediately go there. Instead, his hand starts at my neck and trails down to my breast and then stomach. He takes his time with savoring the curves of my breast and the smoothness of my stomach. He goes lower, and my legs shake gently.

Finally.

He stops just short, and I let out a small whimper.

"Patience, Beauty."

I can feel his mischievous grin. He knows exactly what he is doing to me even though I can't see it.

God, how I want to see him. When I go home, I want to be able to replay this in my head, but I won't be able to visualize him. Not really.

His body presses against me as his lips devour my neck. I silently scream from the intensity that his touch invokes inside me. All he has done is fucking kiss me, and I'm already losing my mind.

Who am I kidding? My mind was lost the second I got that text message.

His hard, thick cock presses against my stomach, and I lose it. I can't wait any longer. I'm done with his slow torture as his hand finds my breast and squeezes my nipple between his fingers. I lift my leg around his body, pressing my entrance to him, hoping he will get the hint that I'm ready. *Now.*

He slaps my ass—hard. I whimper loudly. He promised he wasn't into that kinky, painful stuff. But I find that, despite the pain, the slap turned me on instead of off, like I would have expected.

"That was for disobeying me. Now, spread. Your. Legs."

His voice, although commanding, is also wavering. I can hear the need dripping from his every word.

I smile inside because I can already feel him giving up a

little bit of his control. I've just pushed him to the edge, and now, there is no way he is going to be able to regain his control in the way he wanted.

I lower my leg and slowly spread my legs. He reaches his hand down and touches my entrance. My legs shake as his fingers slowly slip in and out.

"Jesus," I moan through the ball gag.

He removes his hand, and I take one defiant step forward, despite his earlier threats. It's just enough so that his cock is pressed against me again, enough to make him lose the last thread of control that he has been holding on to.

He growls as he grabs my ass, and then he lifts me into the air and brings me down onto his hard cock.

Oh. My. God.

My legs automatically wrap around his body, holding on for dear life. But I quickly realize that he can more than hold my weight as he thrusts inside me, burying himself inside me, in what feels like a challenge that he's somehow won. I've never been fucked like this in my life, and after this, I never want to be fucked any other way again.

"Look at me, Beauty," he says.

I open my eyes, not even realizing when I closed them. Probably the second he entered me, and it was the only thing left I could control. I see him staring back at me, inches from my face, as he continues to torture me below. I'm so close, and the way he is devouring me with his eyes might be my undoing.

In the darkness, I can't tell what color his eyes are, and I don't really care. *Jesus Christ, I don't care.* I could stare into his devastatingly dangerous eyes all night even if we weren't entwined together at the moment. But being able to see this one part of him, as he fucks me, is too much.

He continues staring at me. He continues fucking me, holding on to my ass to keep me from falling, while his other hand reaches up and removes the ball gag from my mouth before dropping it to the floor. I thought, the second that it was gone, I would have all sorts of words to say to this man. But I have no words. All of my words are gone. I can't think of even the simplest of words to say to this man. All that escapes my mouth are a mix of groans, whimpers, and, *Oh my God*s.

Not that he gives me a whole lot of time to speak anyway. His tongue buries itself inside my mouth, like he has been kissing me his entire life. It feels like we have been doing this our entire life. He doesn't feel like a stranger, considering he knows the curves of my body and exactly how to kiss me. The way he knows just how to read my mind. There is only one man in my life who knows me that well.

How did I not see it before?

I pull back from his lips. "Jake?"

He laughs. "I don't know who Jake is, but if I'm reminding you of another guy, then I'm not doing my job right."

That's when everything changes. His intensity. His growls. The way he slaps my ass as he pounds into me. I don't wonder if he is Jake again. I don't really care if he is or isn't. And I can no longer think straight.

Our breathing picks up. Our moans get louder. And our bodies collide faster.

Until I'm coming, and he is shooting his load inside me.

"Fuck, Beast!" I scream as I come.

He doesn't put me back down immediately. Instead, our eyes stay locked on each other as we both try to quiet our breathing. Eyes that I will never forget, that will haunt me all my life.

I quickly realize I can't keep looking at him. I have to forget about this night. If not, I will never move on. This was one night to get lost in and then forget. I can't take it with me.

He slowly lifts me off his cock and then lowers me to the ground. He holds on to me until I've steadied myself on my heels.

And then he's gone.

It gives me time to repeat to myself over and over again, *This is just a dream. This didn't really happen. I didn't just let a stranger fuck me. I have to forget.*

When he returns, I don't know what to expect. If he's looking for another fuck, it will have to wait. My arms ache from being tied over my head, and I can barely stand. I'm exhausted. I need a break before it can happen again—and it *needs* to happen again.

When I feel his hand between my legs, I tense. "I can't—"

"Hush," he says.

That's when I realize what he is doing. He's cleaning me up.

Strange, this man is. Dangerous. Controlling. Dark. Mysterious. And caring? It seems out of character for him.

When he has finished, he removes the rope from my arms. I slowly lower them, afraid that I'm going to collapse from exhaustion. He's got me covered though as he quickly scoops me up in his arms. He carries me to a bed and then places me on it. I don't argue. I don't say anything as he covers me up. I'm too tired to do anything but sleep.

I feel the mattress move as he climbs into bed with me. I'm shocked when his arms go around me. I wouldn't have thought he was the snuggling type, but there is more to my beast of a man than I thought there was.

I feel his cock press against my ass, already hardening, and I freeze. I can't. Not yet.

"Sleep, Beauty. You're going to need your rest for what I have planned for you next."

I take a deep breath, relaxing. "Good night, Beast."

I drift quickly into sleep. I don't worry about what this stranger has done to me or could do to me in my sleep. I don't worry if he used a condom or not when he came inside me. I'm on birth control, and I'll get tested later. I won't be doing anything this stupid again anyway. And I don't wonder if the man holding me is Jake or another ex or a complete stranger. I don't think. I can't because he's taken even that from me.

$$3$$

BEAST

EARLY LIGHT PEEKS in through the blinds, telling me that it is time for me to go. I shouldn't have even stayed for as long as I did. Every minute that passes is another minute that she might wake and find out who I am. Despite how much I want to roll her over and fuck her, I can't. She won't want to fuck me, not after what I did. Not after she realizes who I am.

Still, I can't help but look at my beauty sleep. *So peaceful, so beautiful* are the only words I can think of that describe her. No, that's not right. I can think of a lot of fucking words. *Dangerous. Strong. Intelligent. Smart-mouthed. Disobedient.* And incredibly *stupid* for trusting someone like me.

I don't know what the hell she was thinking. If it weren't me that she'd said yes to, I would have taken her aside and yelled at her until she realized how stupid she was to trust a complete stranger so easily. I could have killed her. I could have done anything I wanted with her. *So stupid!*

I glance down at my sleeping beauty one last time. It has to be the last time. I can't do this again. I can't risk it. I promised myself, if she said yes, then that would be it. That I wouldn't see her again.

And I have to keep that promise to myself.

I slip out of bed and slowly put my clothes on. A small part of me hopes that she will wake up and see me. A small part hopes that I am wrong. That when she sees it is me, she will be happy and want more of me instead of running away in fear. I know that will never happen though, and even if she woke up and saw me and still wanted me, I couldn't let her be in my life. She deserves better than me.

I finish dressing, and then there is nothing left to do but say good-bye and never look back. I stand over her, thinking back to last night. I never woke her again to fuck her. That might have been my biggest fucking mistake, not taking her again while I still had my chance. I couldn't though. Watching her sleep was all I could do. She was too perfect to wake.

I think back to what she called me last night. *Beast*, I think it was. I frown. I don't know why she picked that name for me. It's far too tame for what I am. I wish I were just a Beast. I wish that were all that I was.

I reach down and tuck her gorgeous hair behind her ear so that I can get one last look. Her plump lips still bear the tiniest bit of stain from her red lipstick. I want to stay around and hear her sassy mouth speak to me again. I want those lips wrapped around my cock as I shoot my load down her throat. I want those fuckable lips crushed on mine.

Never again.

I don't tempt myself by kissing those lips. If I do, I will never leave.

Instead, I turn and walk out of her life. "Good-bye, Beauty."

4
___

SCARLETT

I WAKE up to an empty bed. Not surprising. I didn't figure Mr. Mysterious would stick around long enough for me to see him in the light of day. I sigh as I lie in the comfy hotel bed. I don't want to get up. As soon as I do, last night will be nothing but a memory. A *really* good memory.

I smile and know that this smile isn't going to leave my face for the rest of the day. I glance at the clock. It's six thirty. I slept in thirty minutes later than I usually do. I have an hour to head back to my apartment, shower, change, and make it to the office by my usual seven thirty. Or I could call in sick and stay in this bed all day, reliving last night, until I'm supposed to meet Kinsley. I am the boss after all.

What good is it, being the boss, if you can't take a break whenever you want?

I hear my phone vibrating nonstop though, and I know it wouldn't be fair to my employees to stay in bed all day. *And what good would it do anyway?*

He's clearly gone, never to return to my life. It was a one-night stand. Nothing more.

Except it was everything more.

My phone stops for a second but then begins buzzing again. I hop out of bed and instantly regret the motion. *Fuck, I'm sore.* I wasn't expecting that after only one round of fucking. I've certainly gone more than one round with a man before, but none of those times left me feeling this sore.

I push through the feeling and search for my phone. It buzzes again, and on a chair in the corner of the room, I see my purse sitting neatly along with my clothes from last night. Not that I can wear those after he destroyed them. *Shit.* I'm going to have to call someone to get me clothes to wear out of here.

I'll worry about that later.

I grab my phone out of my purse. I already have five missed calls from Preston. More than a hundred unread emails. And a dozen or more text messages from various employees needing answers to their questions. I smile though when I see one from Kinsley.

Kinsley: Can't wait to see ya in a few!

I type my quick response to her, ignoring the rest of the messages until I at least get into work.

Me: Can't wait either! I have some hot news of my own.

Kinsley: Yes! It's been too long since I've gotten to live vicariously through your sex life. I always feel bad about sharing my married hot sex.

I sigh. It's not that I don't like hearing Kinsley's sex stories, but they always revolve around the same man—a man whom I have to see multiple times a year and spend holidays with. It is a little hard to enjoy my Thanksgiving dinner with them after she's told me that Killian fucked her over the dining room table when she was trying to prepare for dinner.

I stop texting Kinsley and look at the dress that is neatly

folded on the chair. I unfold it to see how much damage is done and if I can salvage it at all. My mouth drops when I see the dress. The rip is completely gone.

I'm stunned, trying to think back to last night. *He most definitely ripped the dress in half. So, how did it magically get back in one piece? Did I just dream up the whole encounter last night?*

I look closer, and that's when I see a tag sticking out of the top of the dress. The bastard bought me a new version of the identical dress to the one I was wearing. I don't know when he found the time to do that last night.

Or did he do that earlier, even before I said yes? Was he prepared for any scenario?

I shake my head as I put on my dress and text my driver the address to pick me up so that I can go home and change before heading into work. My driver, George, replies right away. He's more than used to picking me up in strange places. If I were smart, I would just carry a change of clothes in my purse for this exact situation, but there is nothing like going back home and showering in my own shower. I love my shower. And, most of the time, the men end up in my bed, not the other way around.

I run my hand through my wild hair as I look around the room for any signs of who the man was. *Who was my beast?*

I don't see any signs though. It's like he wasn't here. I walk into the living room, and I know it's where he fucked me, but there are no signs of anything that happened here either. The rope is gone. The furniture is perfectly in place. It doesn't even smell like sex in here. But it doesn't stop every feeling from last night from cropping back into me.

I walk to the door and open it without glancing back. I can't glance back. If I do, I will spend the rest of my day in this room, dreaming about a man I can never have again. So, I leave without a good-bye.

My phone rings, and this time, I answer Preston, knowing that work is the only thing that has a chance of distracting me.

"You're late," Preston says as I walk into my office.

I smile at my neurotic assistant. I know I'm not more than ten minutes late. Although unusual for me, it is not a big deal. I reach for my latte that is already sitting on my desk and take a sip. It's already starting to get cold from sitting on my desk for the last ten minutes, not that I really care.

"We have a meeting in twenty minutes with possible new financial managers. Later, you have several meetings to decide on whom the new financial managers are going to be. The designers want you to approve your new eyeshadow line. You need to decide on the final design for the box the shadows will go in.

"Then, you have about a million emails that you need to get through in thirty minutes because you have to meet with the models for the fall line to ensure they are up to your standards.

"You have a lunch with the designer you hired to help with the men's line.

"You have to prep for interviews you have with several magazines first thing tomorrow morning.

"And then you have—"

"Take a breather, Preston. That's why I hired you—to ensure that I am everywhere I'm supposed to be. I don't really need to hear every detail of my schedule for today. Just make sure I'm there. And I already told you to cancel everything after one p.m."

Preston's mouth drops. "I didn't think you were serious. You've never canceled anything before, and you really can't cancel anyway. You have—"

"I have nothing after one today."

Preston's eyes grow large. "Scarlett, that really can't happen. You have—"

"Nothing after one today," I say more sternly.

"But you have to prep and then—"

"I don't need to prep. I've done hundreds of interviews before. I think I can handle tomorrow's without meeting with Cynthia to prep. My lunch meeting is fine, as long as it is done by one. And anything I have scheduled for later, you can handle. That's why I pay you the big bucks."

Preston frowns, although he knows everything I said is true.

If I didn't show up for work for the next year, he could handle everything just as well as I could—if not better. He's been my right-hand man from basically the start. He's the one who keeps me sane and going at work. He knows what decision I'm going to make before I do.

His only flaw is his confidence in himself. As an assistant, he's great. He keeps me in line and will do everything and more. He will stand up for me, no matter the situation. But, when it comes to standing up for himself, the guy lacks balls.

Even when I increased his salary to almost half a million a year, he tried to talk me out of it. He thought I was crazy for giving him that much money, said he was an assistant and I shouldn't pay him that much.

What he doesn't realize is, he is more than just an

assistant. He's *me* when I'm gone. If only I could give him the confidence to actually be me, then I wouldn't have to work the crazy hours that I do. Starting work at seven thirty and then not getting off until ten, just in time to hit up a bar, and then start it all over again is not exactly what I imagined doing all my life when I started this company. I hate to admit it, but I imagined I would be married with kids by this point in my life. Even if I enjoy the one-night stands and putting myself and my company first, I still thought that was where I would be at this point in my life. And if I ever want a chance at having a family at some point, I'm going to need someone I can depend on.

"But I just can't—"

I glare at Preston. "You can. Whatever decisions need to be made after one today are yours to make. I don't want a text message asking me which color is better for the font on an ad. I don't want a phone call saying there is an emergency in shipping. I don't want an email asking if I want to do a press interview. Whatever it is, you handle it!"

Preston sighs. "Yes, Scarlett."

I smile. "Now, let's get to work, so I can go see my best friend."

"The first firm of financial guys are here," Preston says, poking his head into my office.

I sigh as I look at the emails that have piled up on my computer. I've barely even made a dent in them, and now, I have to pause to take a meeting that I don't really care about.

"Okay, let them in," I say, standing from my desk and trying to apply a smile to my face.

I hate interviewing new financial guys. They are always so boring, and I'm afraid they are totally going to burst my happy bubble that I'm in after having the best sex of my life. The fake smile on my face easily turns into a real smile as soon as I let a few memories from last night creep back into my brain.

The rope around my wrists. The feel of his rough hands on my breasts. My legs wrapped around his body.

"Miss Bell, my name is Dustin Morgan, here with guys from Morgan Real Estate. Is now a good time to meet with you?" a man who is suddenly standing in front of me says.

I look from him to Preston, who is standing next to him. He rolls his eyes at me because he knows I was just zoned out when I went back to my one-night stand. It isn't the first time that has happened while I've been at work today, and I know it won't be the last.

"Sorry." I try to lighten the smile on my face, but I can't. "Yes, now is a good time. I'm Scarlett Bell. Nice to meet you..."

"Dustin Morgan," the man says, smiling and extending his hand to me.

I shake it and study the man who looks close to my age. He's wearing an expensive suit, and he has dark black hair and a tight smile.

"These are my associates, Kristopher Bryant and Felix Guild."

"Nice to meet you," I say to both of the men before shaking each one's hand.

His associates seem quiet in comparison to Dustin. I glance to Kristopher, who is good-looking, but there is nothing special about his suit and blond hair. I peek at the last man, Felix. He looks at me with such intensity in his eyes that my heart stops just a little.

I glance back to Dustin, unable to look at Felix without fearing for my life.

At any other time, these three hot men standing in my office would have my full attention. I would be deciding which one I would hire and which one would be in my bed tonight. Not right now though. Now, I can barely concentrate on them because, if I hit on any of them, I know none of them would be able to live up to my experience last night. So, why even bother?

We all take our seats, and then Dustin begins droning on and on about why I should choose his company over any of the others. Thank God for Preston, who keeps the conversation going and asks all the important questions, because I am barely registering any of their words.

I'm back with Beast in the darkness, and that's where I stay for the rest of the day until I leave to go see Kinsley.

5

———

SCARLETT

Georgia drops me off at Eileen's Cheesecake at one thirty p.m. exactly. My smile brightens when I see my best friend already seated at a table with a large cheesecake placed in the middle. I quickly walk over to her, and she stands and immediately hugs me.

"I'm so glad you made it. I wasn't sure until I saw that you were actually here," Kinsley says.

I frown. "I told you I would be here, so I'm here." I glance down at the table as I take a seat opposite her. "I see you've already taken the liberty of ordering an entire cheesecake. I know this is supposed to be about us catching up and all, but I don't think that, even in our best days in college, we could have finished off an entire cheesecake between the two of us."

Kinsley smiles. "I'm hungry, and I will eat an entire cheesecake if I want to. You wouldn't deny a pregnant woman something she was craving, would you?"

I scream, and within seconds, I'm up and out of my seat, crushing my best friend with a hug. "You're really pregnant?" I half-ask and half-squeal.

Kinsley laughs. "Yes, I'm really pregnant, but I would appreciate it if you didn't tell the whole world yet."

"My best friend is pregnant!" I scream to the two other people seated at a table outside the small restaurant.

A few passersby stop and look at me like I'm crazy, but I don't care. She's pregnant.

I go back to my seat, not able to contain my excitement. "How? When?"

Kinsley laughs again. "I think you know how. You see, when two people love each other, the husband sticks his—"

"Stop!" I laugh. "You know what I meant. I thought you said you didn't want children. I thought that was what you and Killian decided was for the best after..." I let my voice trail off, not able to bring those memories back, but it doesn't damper Kinsley's smile.

"That's just what we told everyone to keep them from asking questions or pressuring us. We've been trying to get pregnant again for a long time. And, now, it's finally happened, and I'm far enough along that we should be safe this time."

"How far along?"

"Three months to the day," she says, smiling.

"Three months! Why didn't you tell me sooner?"

"I had a doctor appointment yesterday that gave us the okay to tell everyone. That's why I haven't wanted to see you these past few months. I knew, if I saw you, I wouldn't be able to keep this a secret."

"Well, I'm happy for you and Killian. If anyone deserves it, you do," I say, beaming.

Kinsley slices the cheesecake and places a slice on each of our plates. We each take a bite of our cheesecake at the same time, and we both moan as the rich, cheesy goodness fills our mouths.

"Do you know if it's a boy or girl yet?"

Kinsley smiles. "Nope, and we aren't finding out until the baby is born."

I frown. "Really? I don't think I could handle not knowing. Don't you want to know, so you can decorate and buy gender-specific things? How am I supposed to know what to design and make for my little niece or nephew if I don't know if it is a boy or girl?"

Kinsley laughs in between mouthfuls of cheesecake. This might not be the most nutritious meal for a pregnant woman, but if I get my way, Kinsley is going to be eating food like this all the time, so my niece or nephew will come out all plump and cute-looking.

"After waiting years and thinking my time was almost up for this to happen for us, I think we can wait to find out the gender. All we care about is that the baby is happy and healthy."

I frown. "What do you mean, time was almost up?"

"I'm thirty-two, turning thirty-three in just a few months. By thirty-five, any pregnancy is automatically considered high risk. I've been through enough miscarriages and shots in my ass from in vitro that I wasn't going to risk a high-risk pregnancy on top of all my other issues. I was running out of time."

I nod, letting that sink in.

We are the same age. I haven't thought about settling down with a man for a long time. The last serious boyfriend I had was in college. I thought I would end up married to him, but after we broke up for the millionth time during our senior year, we never got back together. I thought, eventually, I would find someone who would convince me that the whole marriage thing was what I wanted, but so far, the single life has been good to me. I know plenty of women who have had kids in their late thirties or early forties. I never thought it would be an issue until I saw my best friend struggle with infertility issues for years. Just because it happens later in life for some women, it doesn't mean it could happen to me.

But do I even want kids and a husband?

"So, what about your news?" Kinsley asks, studying me.

I lay my fork down even though I'm only halfway through my delicious cheesecake. I'm not sure I really care to eat anymore.

"What news?" I ask.

Kinsley laughs. "The man who had you smiling like an idiot before you found out my news. Who's the guy?"

I freeze, not sure I should really tell Kinsley about last night. She will overanalyze it and convince me it meant something. Persuade me I should text him and ask him out. Convince me that last night could lead to love instead of being what it was—a one-night stand that I will never forget. He has probably already moved on to his next catch for tonight. I'm nothing but a distant memory to him.

"He was nobody. Just another stupid one-night stand."

"I don't believe a word out of your mouth, Scar. Now, spill. That's what you would tell me to do if things were reversed," Kinsley says.

I study her as my smile returns to my face. It was an amazing night, and if I don't tell her, I might burst. Even if it means I will have to deal with her opinions about it being something that it was not. Even if she thinks it was stupid of me and dangerous.

"Okay, okay," I say.

Both of our faces light up with excitement. We're like two schoolgirls who are about to talk about their crushes.

"So, I was sitting at this bar—"

"Two Hundred Sixty-Nine Bar," Kinsley interrupts me, already knowing which bar I'm talking about.

I smile. "Yes. I was sitting there, and of course, no men were at the bar. I mean, *none*. I was drinking my sorrows away, knowing that I wasn't going to be bringing any men home to my bed, when I got a text message."

Kinsley leans forward, listening to my every word. "Who was it?"

"I don't know. The message was from an unknown number. I didn't think the message was for me. But it was."

"What do you mean? Who was it? It had to have been someone you knew if they had your number. Don't keep a pregnant woman in suspense. Just tell me!"

I laugh. "I don't know who it was."

"You didn't ask his name at any point during this?"

"Of course I did. But he didn't want to do names. He just texted me to meet him at the Waldorf, and I did."

Kinsley frowns. "I should so lecture you for meeting a complete stranger in a hotel, but since you are still alive and well, I won't. But don't do it again. My baby needs his or her Aunt Scar."

Kinsley rubs her stomach, and I smile.

"Duly noted. I will not meet a complete stranger in a hotel room again."

"What did he look like?"

"I don't know."

"What the hell, Scar? Did you fuck this guy or not?"

My smile widens at my friend's use of a cuss word. She doesn't cuss often, but when she does, it is by far the most adorable thing on the planet.

"It was dark."

"And you didn't think to turn the lights on?"

"Of course I did, but having the lights off made it better.

More mysterious. He took control from the second I entered the room, and I sort of liked it. It was the best fuck of my life, Kins."

Kinsley sits back in her seat. "So, are you going to see this mysterious-best-fuck-of-your-life guy again?"

I sink into my chair, hating my answer, but having to say it anyway because I already know the answer to that question. It's an answer that I've been avoiding since I woke up this morning.

"No, I'm not going to see him again."

To my surprise, Kinsley doesn't have a reply to that.

Who I am kidding?

She completely has a reply but just isn't telling me.

"Come on, tell me what you are thinking, oh wise one."

Kinsley smiles. "I'm not saying anything. This is something you are going to have to figure out on your own."

I sigh and then look up, and I see Killian walking toward us with a serious grimace on his face.

"Hey, Kill! Congrats on finally knocking up your wife," I say, getting out of my chair to give him a hug.

He hugs me, and when I let him go, I see the tiniest bit of a smile slip onto his lips.

He turns to Kinsley, who hops out of her seat and smiles at her husband. He instantly smiles back and takes her into his arms, possessively holding her while he holds on to her stomach.

"You have a good meeting, babe?" Kinsley asks.

"Not really, but seeing you makes everything better, princess," Killian says to his wife. Then, he firmly kisses her on the lips.

My heart warms every time I see them together. And, now, they are having a baby. God, they are such grown-ups. And they couldn't look happier.

It's what I want, a little voice in my head says.

I shake my head. *No way. I love running my empire. I love...*

Except what if running an empire isn't enough anymore?

Maybe that's why, even when I find a new man to fuck every night, it is never enough to keep me satisfied for more than a day.

Except last night was enough. If I had that every night, I wouldn't care if I were married with a baby on the way.

But most one-night stands are not like last night.

What if I want marriage? What if I want to have a baby before it's too late? What if I want everything Kinsley has?

I sigh. The problem is, I don't really know what I want, and I hate that because, usually, I know exactly what I want. I always thought, when I was ready to settle down and start a family, there would be a clear sign pointing me that way.

Maybe Kinsley being pregnant is that sign?

6

———

BEAST

My PHONE BUZZES, and I jump to pull it out of my pocket, hoping that it's her. I glare at my phone when I see that it's not her.

I answer the call but don't bother saying hello.

"We have a job for you."

"I thought I was already in the middle of the most important job I could have."

"Yes, well, now, we have another for you."

"What's the pay?"

He laughs. "Really? You used to never care about pay. It used to be all about the thrill of the chase. Thrill of doing something you love. I didn't know you had changed so much."

He damn well knows why everything has changed. I'm not going to sit here and fucking explain it to him.

"What's. The. Pay?" I spit my words out.

He laughs again. "Come in and find out for yourself, but you know she's not going to be happy if you turn the job down."

I end the call. I don't need him fucking reminding me

how pissed *she's* going to be if I don't take the job. I already fucking know.

So much for having an easy, relaxing day.

I walk over and pull a suit out of the closet. Even when I'm supposed to have a day off, I never get a day off. After these jobs are over, I need to take a vacation. I need to forget about my fucked up life for a while and just disappear. Maybe think about changing professions even.

In the meantime, I have to find a better way to deal with this tension.

I pull out my phone and text something I shouldn't.

7

SCARLETT

UNKNOWN: I know you are thinking about me.

Me: I am not. I don't even know who this is.

Unknown: You're thinking, "How could a stranger turn me on so much? How could a stranger know me so well?"

Me: You're right. It's because I don't think you are a stranger at all.

I turn my phone off. He shouldn't be texting me. I thought it was only supposed to be one night. I can't let him think that it is going to be anything more. I can't let him pull me back into the temptation of having him more than one night when I know it's not going to lead to anything else but dissatisfaction with every other man.

Not after I've realized I want more than just one night with him. In order to satisfy my thirst for him, I would need night after night after night for years. And, even then, I'm not sure I would have enough of him. And if I can't have that, then I want something more meaningful than one-night stands that will never live up to him. I want something that could lead to marriage and babies. That might be the only way to forget about him.

"Scarlett!" Preston says as he knocks on the door to my office.

I motion for him to enter. He does, and I watch as the door swings shut behind him.

"Why is your phone turned off?"

I stare down at my phone that I just turned off and laid on my desk. "Because I'm trying to ignore a one-night stand who won't go away."

Preston rolls his eyes. "You can block people's numbers, you know. You don't need to turn your phone off."

"What's up?" I ask, not willing to tell him that I can't block his number. I don't have the self-control to do that because I want him to text me.

"You have a meeting with the new financial guy in five minutes."

"What financial guy?"

Preston slumps into the chair in the corner of the office. I raise my eyebrows at him. I've never seen him so flustered on the job before. He is always the epitome of professional.

I stand up from behind my desk and move to the chair next to him, taking a seat. "What's going on, Preston?"

"I can't handle this! You can't just leave me in charge on such short notice again. Do you know how many decisions I had to make yesterday? About a million."

I laugh as Preston continues rambling.

I know the feeling. I make about a million decisions a minute.

"I just can't handle it. This is not what I signed up for when I took this job as your assistant. I am supposed to be *assisting* you, not making the decisions myself. I've taken a whole container of Pepto and antacids, trying to calm my stomach. But I'm a nervous wreck.

"I had to finalize the colors for your new eye shadow,

pick the model who is going to be featured in your new makeup ad campaign, interview a financial manager since our last one retired, plan your schedule for today without you. It's just..." Preston whips his head to look at me. "I have a life, too, you know. I have a girlfriend whom I promised to take out to a late dinner, but I had to cancel on her, and—"

"Wait!" I raise my eyebrows at him. "You have a girlfriend?" I spit out without even thinking.

I always just assumed Preston was gay, like ninety percent of the men who work for me. He's a petite, scrawny-looking man, whose favorite thing in the world is fashion. He usually wears skinny jeans and a tight-fitting shirt. Depending on the trends, his hair changes just as fast as his clothes, but right now, he is a blond, his hair spiked up in the center with the sides shaved. Occasionally, I've even seen him wear a little makeup.

I had no idea he had a girlfriend.

Preston rolls his eyes at me. "I know, I know. You thought I was gay. I'm not."

How many times have I gotten completely naked in front of this man because I thought he was gay? How many dirty details from my sexual encounters have I overshared with him?

I shrug. *Oh well.*

"It's not that exactly. It's just...I have never heard you..." I stop when I see Preston staring at me, like he knows I thought he was gay, and there is no point in denying it. He's right, so I stop. "Okay, you caught me. I thought you were gay, but to my defense, you never corrected me or talked about a girlfriend before."

"That's because we have only been dating for two weeks, and I don't think it is very professional to bring up home situations at work."

I smile at my workaholic assistant. "You must think I'm a terrible boss then because that is all I talk about."

Preston shakes his head. "You're the boss. You are allowed to talk about anything you want."

"So are you! Preston, you've been with me for almost eight years now. I don't think of you as just my assistant. I think of you as one of my closest friends. You've spent Thanksgiving with me for the last three years, for God's sake. Please stop acting like you are just like any other employee. Get some balls, and get over not being able to make decisions. You can so make decisions as well or even better than me.

"Now, tell me about this new girlfriend."

Preston blushes, but then his phone buzzes in his pocket, and he jumps up. "The new financial guy is here. I'll see him in."

I sigh and get up as well. I slowly walk over to my desk, not excited to hear what the new financial guy Preston hired has to say. I'm sure he's great. I know Preston wouldn't hire anyone who wasn't anything less than amazing. Still, talking with financial guys is not the highlight of my day. I would rather think about clothes and makeup or, better yet, how I'm going to find me a husband. Not talk about the business's finances, which I already know are better than fine.

"I want a rain check though on hearing about the girlfriend, Preston!" I shout to him as he leaves my office.

I glance down at my phone that is still dark, sitting on my desk. I consider turning it back on and checking to see if *he* texted. From just thinking about what he might have texted me, my nipples harden to attention beneath the white dress I'm wearing that scoops low in the middle. My finger hovers over the On button when a knock sounds at my door.

The door swings open again, and Preston pokes his head in.

"This is Mr. Jake Walton, senior financial manager," Preston says.

My mouth drops as Jake appears in my doorway. *What the hell? This has to be a joke.*

I haven't seen Jake since I broke it off with him in college.

Jake, on the other hand, doesn't seem surprised at all that I'm who he is visiting today. He smirks a little when he sees me staring at him with my mouth half-open, and then his eyes lock on my hard nipples that are very visible beneath the thin white material. He probably thinks they are hard because of him and not because of a possible text message from a stranger. Never in my life had I wished more that I had worn a bra.

"I've got it from here, Preston. Scarlett and I go way back," Jake says.

Preston stares in horror from Jake to me. He knows he has fucked up, but I can't let him think that. I want him to feel confident in his decisions. I'm sure Jake is a very competent financial manager. In the future, I just need to give Preston a list of all my ex-boyfriends and one-night stands, so he doesn't accidentally hire one again.

Preston mouths the word, *Sorry.*

I shake my head, doing my best to smile at him, and then he slumps out of my office, closing the door behind himself.

"Well, that was deceptive. There are other ways to get a girl to go out with you, you know, Jake. You can't just trick my assistant into hiring you and think that I will go out with you."

Jake grins again as he takes a seat in the chair in front of my desk even though I didn't invite him to. "Are you finished?"

"What?"

"Are you finished? I didn't come here to ask you out. I have a fiancée. My firm assigned me to your company after Lloyd Mayor retired. And I was supposed to have an interview with you yesterday anyway. I thought you would take one look at me and want someone else. That's why I requested this meeting with you personally today. I didn't want you to think I was taking advantage of you not being at the interview yesterday."

He has a fiancée, is all I hear. He has a fiancée.

The man's a dick. He came here, and that is the first thing out of his mouth. He has to flaunt it to me that he has a fiancée while I have nothing.

My inner voice reminds me, *That isn't true.*

I have an entire company while he, I'm sure, makes decent money while working at a financial firm, but it is nothing compared to what I have.

"So, are you okay with me being your financial manager?" Jake asks.

I fold my arms over my chest as I study Jake. He looks almost exactly the same as he did in college. Light-brown hair tamed nicely on top of his head; brown eyes that say, *Take me home to mama*, without an ounce of danger lurking behind them; clean-shaved face; and a nice suit that could use a little more tailoring to show off his muscles that seem to have gotten larger since the last time I saw him.

"Yes."

Jake smiles, and I see the tension that I must have missed seep out of his eyes. He thought I would say no. Like I have a chance of that happening now. I have to at least appear that I am over him. Because I was. Before he walked in that door, I was completely over him. I have barely thought about him since I broke up with him during our senior year of college. He's too perfect. He always wanted the American dream—married with two kids on the way. A wife who would stay home with the kids. I didn't want any of those things back then.

But now…

Now, that might be exactly what I need to move on from the best sex of my life. It might be exactly what is missing from my life.

I crook my head to one side as I look at him. He's good-looking; he always has been. And even though I don't ache for him to rip off my clothes and take me like animals do, even though I don't remember the sex to be anything special, I still want him. I want the dream. I think back to the first time I saw him in college. I was getting out of a class and he was horsing around playing touch football with several guys in the open field between buildings. I remember stopping to watch. Half of the men were shirtless after all. But it wasn't just his body that caught my attention. It was his confidence, his smile. After I saw that I didn't give him a choice but to go out with me. He was and still is an all-around good guy. He's the exact type of guy who can give me my own happily ever after. Instead of daydreaming about one-night-stand guy, I should be convincing Jake to marry me and give me everything I never knew I wanted.

"Marry me?" I spit out without thinking.

Jake's eyes widen when I say the words, but he doesn't laugh or immediately tell me no. He's too nice of a guy to do either of those things.

"I have a fiancée," he says again, like that's a reason for not being able to say yes.

He hasn't married her yet, and as far as I'm concerned,

he must not be that into her if he is here with me. If he didn't want to jeopardize his relationship with her, he wouldn't be here with me.

"So?" I run my tongue over my bottom lip.

He glares at me. "How about I take you out for dinner as two friends, and you can tell me what's going on?"

My lips curl up into a tight smile. "Yes."

8

BEAST

ME: *You want more than one night. Admit it. You want more. You want to take my cock between your fucking lips until I shoot cum down your throat. You want to know how it would feel to take me in your ass. You want it all. Admit it.*

"Are you listening? Put your damn phone away!" my boss shouts at me.

"Yes, sir. I'll arrange a meeting for the day after tomorrow, and the job will be done by the end of the week."

"Good. Don't fuck this up, son. You've fucked up too many things already."

I glare at him. "I'm the best. That's why you are sending me."

"You are also the only one who has royally fucked up everything before."

I abruptly stand up, knocking my chair backward. "Then, send someone else if you think I'm a fuckup. I quit!"

I storm out of his office and head toward the stairs. I need to take the stairs down the ten flights to try to cool off. Plus, I know I won't make it out of this building without him sending someone to remind me why I can't quit. Because he owns me.

Fuck.

I look down at my phone and begin typing again. I thought just texting her would quiet the desires she spurs inside me. I was wrong.

9

SCARLETT

I DON'T BOTHER CHANGING for my date with Jake tonight. I already know the white dress that I'm wearing is perfect for seducing a man. From the stares I have gotten all day from the few straight men who work for me, I know it's a hit. And I don't want Jake to think I'm desperate because I'm not. I'm the furthest thing from desperate.

I didn't even think about *him* as I went about my work today. Okay, that's not true. When I wasn't thinking about Jake, I was thinking about the mysterious stranger who shouldn't have texted me back. I still haven't turned my phone back on to see if he sent me any other messages, but it didn't keep me from thinking about him every second I got.

I'm thinking about *him* as I contemplate turning my phone back on when I hear Jake's voice stir me back to reality.

"It's eight thirty. You ready for dinner yet, or do you need to work some more? I'm fine either way. I have plenty of work to keep me busy if you aren't ready yet."

I glance at the clock on my office wall. *How did it get so late so fast?* I still have hours' worth of work, but I should call it a night. I run a hand through my hair, loosening it from this morning even more.

"Yeah, I guess I should call it quits," I say even though I feel like I should work longer, especially after ducking out yesterday to spend time with Kinsley. "I just need to tell Preston that I'm heading out, and he should go home," I say.

Jake nods, and I walk past him to Preston's office, which is next door to mine.

His door is already open, so I just have to poke my head in. "Go home."

Preston lifts his head from the computer he is working on. "I will soon. I just need to—"

"No. Go home to that girlfriend of yours, and take her on that date you missed because of me."

Preston nods but doesn't get up from his computer. I walk over and unplug it, not caring what damage is done to the computer or what info he will lose that he didn't save.

"Shit, Scarlett. I was working on your schedule for tomorrow. I still need to send a couple of more emails."

"No, you don't. Go home, Preston."

I wait and watch as he gathers his things and then leaves with a scowl on his face. I walk back to my office, passing Jake, who is standing in the doorway with his arms folded over his chest, smirking at me. I ignore him as I walk to my desk to grab my purse and things.

"You're one bossy boss. Should I be worried you are going to boss me around, like you did him?" Jake teases.

I glance up at him. "Yes," I answer honestly because I already know I'm a bossy woman.

He steps forward. "You are the most intimidating woman I know. It's one of the reasons you and I never worked out. You're too much woman for me, Scarlett."

I bite my lip as he says my name. He's one of the few people who always called me Scarlett instead of shortening it. No matter how long we dated, I was always Scarlett, never Scar.

"I'll work on the intimidation thing."

Jake laughs. "Yeah, you work on that."

"I will."

He laughs again. "You can't change who you are. You're bossy, controlling, intimidating, and sexy as hell. That's who you are, Scarlett."

I smile as I walk past him.

"What's the devious grin for?" Jake asks.

"You called me sexy. That means, there is hope yet."

"Now, just wait a minute. I didn't mean—"

I wink at him. "Come on. Let's go on our *date*."

"Scarlett, I already told you, it's not a—"

I turn and suddenly kiss him on the cheek, shutting him up.

I'm going to marry him. He might not agree yet, but he is exactly what I need—stable, ambitious, settled. He wants to get married and have babies, and he already knows everything about me. He's exactly what I need.

10

SCARLETT

"So, where are you taking me?" I ask.

"I was going to leave it up to you. You never let me choose where we went before. Why would I think tonight was going to be any different?"

I frown. I know that I'm bossy and usually in control, but maybe I always took control because he never did, no matter how much I desperately wanted him to.

"Well, I'm letting you choose everything we do tonight. I don't want to have to make another decision the rest of the night. I'm leaving everything up to you—from where we go to what I order to whether or not you take me home and fuck me later."

Jake frowns and gives me a dirty look at that last one.

"Relax. I said you get to decide that one," I say, winking, as we head out of the elevator of Beautifully Bell Enterprises.

It doesn't wipe the frown from his face or relax his tense shoulders beneath his suit that isn't the least bit wrinkled, despite him working in it all day long. I glance down at my own dress that has a few wrinkles in it and even a small stain near the hem that I don't know where it came from. Even his ordinary life is perfect compared to mine.

"So, where are we going?" I ask again as we exit the building. I consider calling my driver to come take us somewhere, but I'm going to let him guide our evening, so I don't.

Jake thinks for a minute, considering where, and then throws out the name of one of the most expensive steak houses in New York City.

I raise my eyebrows at his suggestion, but he's the one deciding, so I just answer, "Sounds good to me."

We begin walking two blocks before I can't stand waiting for him to figure out that we sure as hell aren't walking the thirty blocks from here to that steak house.

"Are you going to hail a cab, or do I need to call my driver?"

"Neither. I'm driving."

"You own a car? In New York City? Who does that?"

He smiles. "Me."

He turns us into a parking garage and walks over to a black Honda Civic.

I sigh. Of course the man I want to marry doesn't even have a nice car.

I climb into the very sensible car as Jake climbs into the driver's seat. It's not that I need a man to have lots of money and expensive things. Despite running a beauty and fashion empire, I'm not overly materialistic. Okay, I am, but I can buy my own nice things. I just want him to buy nice things for himself, too. Especially when I know how much I am paying him, so he can easily afford more than this car on the salary I am paying him alone. And I know I'm not his only client, so he makes more than enough to own a nicer car.

"Nice car," I say in a snarky voice.

"Thank you," he says, ignoring my snark.

The car ride to the restaurant is long. Neither of us talks, and Jake doesn't bother turning the radio on to drown out the silence. He probably enjoys the silence, thinks it's calming. I hate the silence. I consider taking out my phone and seeing if I have any more messages, but I don't. I'm going to give Jake everything I've got.

When we pull up to the steak house, Jake valets his car. I smile when I see the valet, who is used to parking expensive Mercedes and Teslas, climb into his car to go park it.

Jake holds open the door to the restaurant, and I walk inside. We are seated at a table almost immediately. The waiter comes over shortly after we are seated. "Can I get you anything to drink?" the waiter asks, looking at me. I turn my attention to Jake. "I'm letting my date for tonight decide," I say, smiling as sweetly as I can.

"Excellent. Sir, what are we having? I can recommend some wine, if you would like," the waiter says.

That's when I realize that Jake might not order wine or alcohol at all. I don't think I can survive tonight without a drink. I need a drink.

Order the wine, I think over and over in my head. I hope that Jake will get the hint that wine is what I need.

Jake smiles at me. "No need for recommendations. I was here about a month ago when I proposed. If I remember correctly, your Stag's Leap Cask 23 wine was an excellent choice. We will share a bottle of that."

The waiter's eyes brighten. "Congratulations," he says to the two of us before he runs off to get us our wine.

I smile as Jake frowns at how his plan backfired so magnificently. He brought me here to remind me that this is where he brought his fiancée. To make me jealous. To make me realize that he is serious, and it will never happen between us. He didn't count on the waitstaff playing right into my hands though.

"So, what is your fiancée's name?"

"Karissa."

"And? Give me details. How did you meet? What does she do? How'd you fall in love? Favorite sex position? Something."

To my surprise, Jake smiles at the last one. Maybe he is capable of lightening up a little bit.

"She's in finance as well. We met when she joined the firm as a financial analyst almost three years ago. She is now the best financial manager—after me, of course. While at a company retreat in Florida about six months after she joined, we fell in love. And doggy style is definitely my favorite."

I spit my water out when he answers my last question. Maybe he isn't as sweet and innocent as he used to be. Maybe there is a layer of danger lurking beneath what he shows the world.

The waiter brings us our wine, and then Jake orders us each a steak, and I'm surprised he remembers how I like it. I taste the wine, and it is delicious.

"What about you?"

I give him a confused look.

"Have any guys found themselves under the control of Scarlett Bell, or have you stomped on any hearts lately?"

"I don't stomp on men's hearts."

"You stomped on mine," he says suddenly, to my surprise.

"I'm sorry."

He shrugs. "It's old news. What I want to know is, why did you suddenly propose to me in your office? What's going on?"

I take another sip of my wine, so I don't have to answer him.

"Scarlett?"

"I've just finally realized it's what I want. I want everything that you have. I want to be married, I want kids, I want to be in love. I always thought having the amazing career would be enough. It's just not enough anymore."

Jake sits back, smiling and nodding. "You deserve all of those things."

"I just can't have those things with you?"

He nods. "I'm not that guy for you. I wish I were. If you had asked me three years ago, I would have said yes so fast. You were the one who got away, Scarlett."

"It's not too late," I say, hopeful, even though I know it is. It's too late. I shouldn't even be asking him to consider me when he has already proposed.

"It's not too late for you to find Mr. Perfect, Scarlett. It's too late for us though."

I sigh. "I know. I just have no idea how to go about finding Mr. Perfect, as you called him."

Jake laughs. "I wouldn't worry about that. As soon as the world finds out you are looking for something more than just one night, guys will be lining up to marry you. You are quite a catch, you know, even if you are intimidating."

"Thanks."

We finish eating while talking about nonsense things. The weather. Trips we have both enjoyed. Our careers. We don't mention my lack of a love life or his fiancée again.

"I can pay," I say when the waiter drops off our bill.

"Not a chance," Jake says sternly to me. "This was my last chance to take out the famous Scarlett Bell. I'm not letting you pay even if you are worth millions more than me."

I smile. "Thanks, Jake. I'm going to head to the ladies' room then. Excuse me."

He nods as I leave the table and head to the restroom. I immediately pull out my phone and turn it on. I have four missed text messages from *him*. I read through to the last one.

Unknown: Admit it, and I'll give you what you want. Admit it, and I'll find you.

Unknown: I know I'm already consuming your every thought. I know you want me to rip off that white dress you're wearing today. I saw your nipples piercing through the thin fabric. Your nipples grew hard because of me. I'm not a patient man. Just say the word.

Unknown: I know what you are doing. You are trying to resist the temptation. You are trying to pretend like the other night didn't happen. You are wrong to try. You can't resist. That night was just the beginning. I can give you so much more.

Unknown: He's not right for you. He wouldn't know what to do with a woman like you, Beauty. Just tell me yes, that you want me to remind you why you can't get me out of your head. Just tell me yes, and I will show you a whole new world you've never conquered before. Just say yes...

Me: Yes.

11

BEAST

BEAUTY: Yes.

Beauty: Where should I meet you?

I can't help but smile at my Beauty. She came to me last time, and now, it's my turn. It's my turn to capture her in the dark. And I can't wait to have her with Jake in the next room. I can't stand watching her go home with him, not until I have her first.

I walk deliberately past him, but he doesn't even glance up from his phone that he is staring at with a frown on his face. I've been watching him all evening, and I don't understand why he hasn't already made his move.

If I were here, having dinner with her, it wouldn't have lasted long. I wouldn't have been able to keep my hands from her hands. I wouldn't have been able to keep from undressing her with my eyes. And she wouldn't have been able to resist my look, knowing that I was going to undress her the second I got out of here. We wouldn't have lasted five minutes at dinner without needing each other again.

I turn my back to him and keep walking, forgetting about that bastard. I have more important things to worry about at the moment. Unlike him, I don't plan on squandering this moment. I plan on taking her. I plan on controlling her. I plan on devouring her.

I head straight to the restroom I know she's already in, most likely fantasizing about where she's supposed to meet me. I push the door open to the women's restroom, immediately turn off the lights, and lock the door behind me.

She doesn't scream, like most women would. Instead, she stiffens. She knows it's me, despite not seeing me, but she doesn't say a word. She doesn't have to. I already know what she's thinking. I know what she wants, and I plan on giving it to her.

"Miss me, Beauty?"

I watch in the mirror and am able to make out the faintest of her movements despite the darkness. My eyes, I suspect, adjust faster than hers. I've always been able to see easier than most in the dark. I watch as she runs her tongue across her lower lip, and then she slowly and deliberately moves her tongue to her upper lip, like she thinks I need some enticement before I fuck her. She doesn't need to know I'm already more than enticed, and I know just what to do.

"You didn't answer me, Beauty. Did. You. Miss. Me?"

"Yes," she breathes, slightly turning her head in my direction.

What I didn't expect is what she does next.

She doesn't bother turning around to face me as her hands move to the straps on her dress, lowering them down her shoulders. Her hand then moves to the back of her dress. She grabs the zipper with one hand and the top of her dress with the other, and then she begins to slowly pull the zipper down her back. I can't take my eyes off of her hand as she lowers the zipper until it stops just above the curve of her ass. I'm entranced by the small of her back as she slowly reveals her smooth skin to me. I can't take my eyes off of her.

I thought I knew this woman, but seeing her undress herself without me even asking might be the sexiest thing I've ever seen.

I growl when the dress drops to the floor in a heap at her feet. She's not wearing underwear again.

God, this woman, I moan silently to myself. *This wonderful, competent, sexy woman.*

She is going to be the death of me. And I'm going to enjoy dying slowly at her hands.

I walk over to her and immediately place my hands on her body. My hands continue moving all over her body, exploring, studying, learning every curve. I grab her neck, pulling her backward, so that I can kiss her while my hands find her breasts. She moans so softly in my grasp that I can barely hear her. It's like she's in a trance the second I touch her. And only I will be able to break the spell I've started.

"Haven't you learned yet that I'm the one who's supposed to tell you what to do?"

"Then, tell me," she says.

I gather her hair in my hands and pull so that her ear is right against my lips. "Put your hands on the counter and spread your legs."

She touches her throat, like she is trying to catch her breath, as my words seem to go in one ear and out the other. She doesn't move to obey me. But she won't get what she wants if she doesn't obey me.

"Now, Beauty." I slap her ass to remind her that I don't like being disobeyed. "Or I won't be able to give you what you want."

She stumbles forward, just barely grabbing ahold of the

counter to keep herself from falling. She quickly regains her composure though as she spreads her legs and arches her back so that her ass is high in the air, begging me to give her what she wants. *And who am I not to give her everything she desires?*

The door to the restroom pushes against the lock, and I watch as Beauty jumps when she hears someone at the door. I smile because I know now that her heart isn't just racing for me; it's racing at the thought of getting caught in the act. I can see her short, shallow panting speed up as she waits for me to fuck her. I can see the liquid dripping down between her legs, begging for me to enter her. And I know, with each second that passes, she is going to grow heavier with need.

I begin slowly undressing, deliberately wanting to take this slow, but I know that I don't have enough time to enjoy her like I want. I undo my belt buckle on my pants and take my cock in my hand, quickly pulling a condom over my shaft. A cock that has been begging for her, begging to feel her wrapped around it again since that night.

I find her eyes in the reflection in the mirror. I know she can't really see me. I know her vision isn't good enough yet in the darkness to make out more than the whites in my eyes, although after a few more minutes her eyes will adjust. But I can see her. And her eyes say everything. Desire. Need. Longing. Wanting.

Jesus, the look is enough to undo a man.

I tangle my hand in her hair, pulling gently to ensure that I can keep looking at her gorgeous big eyes as I enter her. My cock rubs against her ass, begging for entrance. As I rub against her, she tilts her ass higher, begging for me to take her already.

I shouldn't do it. I shouldn't claim her ass, not like this.

Not before ample prep. Not when I promised that I wouldn't hurt her. But my need to conquer all of her beats out the pain I might cause her since tonight might be my last chance to have her this way.

I don't give her any warning other than the tug of her hair as I drive my cock into her ass. She's tight—*God, she's tight*—as I drive inside her. I lock eyes with hers, looking for any hint of fear or pain, but there is none, only increased desire. Her lips are parted, and her cheeks are flushed, but I read nothing that says she hates me or wants me to stop.

"Good girl," I say as I begin moving inside her.

"Oh my God," she says.

Her words would be enough to undo me if I hadn't expected them and had already stopped to prevent myself from becoming completely undone.

I move again, and this time, it's with ravaged, fast-paced, unable-to-control-myself-any-longer thrusts. She matches me thrust for thrust, unable to control herself as well.

There is no speaking. Neither of us could if we wanted to. There are barely any groans or moans escaping her lips, most likely for fear of being heard. There is just us moving as one until we are both coming as one.

I collapse on top of her back, not able to keep myself from feeling all of her against my skin, if only for a second.

Fuck, I don't understand what this woman is doing to me. I don't understand how, even after I just had her, I still want her. That's never happened to me before. I've fucked countless women and never even thought about looking back after I left. But I know, after leaving her, it's going to be hard not to look back.

But I have to. This has to be the end. I have a job to do, and she would just complicate things.

I remove myself from her and find her dress on the floor as I tuck myself back into my pants. She stands slowly.

I toss the dress to her. "Get dressed, Beauty."

"You know, one of these times, you should let me be in control," she says with a grin slowly spreading over her face.

"Not a chance." *Because this isn't happening again.*

I unlock the door and walk out of the restroom before she has a chance to say something that'd make me change my mind.

12

SCARLETT

"You've got that goofy grin on your face again," Preston says as he walks into my office.

"So?" I ask, still smiling. From last time, I know that it's not going to disappear easily. I take a sip of my latte as I wait for Preston to continue.

"So your not-a-date with Mr. Walton turned into another one-night stand to add to your endless list?"

I frown. "No. He's engaged. I don't break up people who are serious about each other."

Preston sighs. "So then, who was it?"

"One-night-stand guy from before," I say.

Preston raises his eyebrows. "Really?"

"Yes. What's so shocking about that?"

"Nothing," Preston says, smiling. He begins to walk toward my door to exit.

"Is that all you came in here to say? To ridicule me for smiling about a guy I had sex with more than once?"

"No. I came to tell you that Mr. Walton requested an appointment with you this afternoon. Apparently, you made quite the impression on him."

I roll my eyes. "Please refer to Mr. Walton as Jake. And I did not. As I said before, he's engaged. And, as you might well have already guessed, Jake and I dated before, and it didn't work out. There's nothing between us."

"Sure, there's not." He disappears before I can say more.

Damn it! What could Jake want?

We've already discussed the business situation, so I doubt he has more to say there. I think for a minute. Probably has to do with taking time off for the wedding. I let whatever it is with Jake go. I have too much work to do today to worry about him—or my mysterious stranger, my Beast.

I just know there's not a chance in hell I'll be able to get him out of my head today, no matter how hard I try. I take out my phone and text him because I can't stand it if that was our last time.

Me: If it's possible, last night might have been better than the first. But I'm greedy. I want more. I want my chance to control your body like you have controlled mine. I think it's your turn to say yes.

I immediately turn my phone off after I send the text. He will text me later, and I will be happy to see his response. But, if I leave my phone on, I will be constantly checking it, and I won't get any work done. Instead, I will just have to settle on dreaming about his response.

I balance a pile of eye-shadow palettes in one hand with a stack of designs in the other as I walk with Preston back to my office. I feel my phone buzz in my pocket, and I immediately think it's *him.*

I realized quickly that having my phone turned off did nothing to help keep Beast out of my thoughts. And it annoyed Preston to death because he couldn't forward my calls to me. So, I ended up turning it back on. The only downside is, now, every time it buzzes, I think it's *him*.

"Preston, can you—"

"Already on it," Preston says as he reaches into my back pants pocket and pulls out my phone. "Miss Bell's office. Preston speaking."

Preston casually says his speech as we continue walking toward my office. I frown because I know it's not *him*. He's never called me before, only texted.

"Yes, she's right here," he says.

I sigh as Preston holds the phone up to my ear. "This is Scarlett."

"Miss Bell, we need to set up a meeting for you to approve the new lipstick colors," Teresa, head of my beauty department, says.

I give Preston a dirty look because this is something he should be handling, not me. But I answer anyway, "I have a meeting that I need to get to right now, but I can meet you in about an hour. Sound good?"

"Yes, Miss Bell, that will work fine."

"Good-bye."

Preston removes the phone from my ear. I'm just about to rip into him when we reach the door to my office, and I see Jake sitting somberly in the chair across from my desk that's angled so he can watch the door waiting for me to enter. I don't know what's happened, but I've seen that face before—on the day I broke up with him—and I know it's not good. I feel the eye-shadow palettes slipping from my grasp, dropping to the floor, one by one, until I'm only holding one. The designs in my other hand scatter to the floor as well. I don't care about either as I step forward toward Jake, who is looking down at the ground.

He looks up as I approach.

I attempt to smile, but it's fake. "What's wrong?"

Jake looks from me to Preston and then back to me, but he doesn't answer.

"Preston, can you give us a minute?"

Preston is already on the floor, trying to gather up the dropped eye shadows and designs. "Just give me one sec—"

"Now!" I say firmly.

"Okay, okay." Preston leaves the items on the floor and shuts the door behind himself, leaving me and Jake alone.

"What's wrong?" I ask as I walk around to the other side of my desk and take a seat, trying to give Jake some space.

"Karissa broke up with me."

My mouth drops open, but I don't know what to say. I feel horrible, as if it has anything to do with me. *It can't though, can it? We didn't do anything wrong.*

I wait for him to say more. I wait for him to explain. He doesn't though. Instead, he just stares at me with bleakness over his face.

"Why?"

Jake frowns.

"It wasn't because of me, was it?"

"No," Jake says.

I wait for more, but he doesn't give me anything.

That's when I realize that Jake might be uncomfortable with having this conversation in his boss's office, and that is the last thing he should be worrying about. He shouldn't feel like I'm his boss—at least not right now. Right now, I'm a friend who is comforting her friend. Nothing more.

I get up from my desk without saying a word to Jake. I

walk past him and open the door leading out into the hallway.

"I need you to cancel the rest of my day."

"What? Why? I can't do that again." Preston gets up from behind his desk, trying to do his best to convince me to stay.

"I can't. Jake needs me."

"What could he possibly need you for?"

"His fiancée just broke up with him."

"Oh," is all Preston says. Then, he laughs.

"What's so funny?" My voice is stern, not finding the fact that Jake's fiancée just broke up with him funny at all.

"There was no fiancée. He just made that all up to get into your panties."

"Just cancel my plans for the rest of the day." I walk out the door and back to my office before Preston has a chance to change my mind. I poke my head back inside my office. "Come on, Jake, let's go. I'm taking you for drinks."

13

SCARLETT

"I'll take a beer," Jake says.

I shake my head at the bartender.

"We'll both take a double scotch on the rocks," I say to the bartender. I turn to Jake. "Beer isn't strong enough to get the job done today, I don't think."

"You're probably right. Since when did you start drinking scotch though?"

The bartender sets both of our drinks on the bar, and I pick up the scotch. It's not as bad as I remember it being.

"Right now," I say as I smile.

Jake attempts to smile again this time, and it isn't as pathetic as the one he gave me in my office. I watch as he takes a sip of the golden liquid. I watch Jake swallow, and his Adam's apple bobs up and down as the liquid goes down his throat. I'm supposed to be here to cheer Jake up, but instead, all I can think about is how I wish I were kissing that throat. And it doesn't help that being in a bar reminds me of the first time I stepped foot in a bar with Jake ten years ago.

"Really? You got me a beer?" I ask.

He smiles bashfully as he slides the beer to me across the small pub table that we are both standing at. I grab the bottle and lift it to my lips. "Good thing I'm not like most girls and can actually drink beer."

He raises his eyebrows at me as if he isn't sure.

I raise my beer and he does the same clinking the bottles together. "To a fantastic first date," I say.

He nods and then I put the beer to my lips. It's not that I don't like beer I just prefer a stronger drink. You get drunk faster with less calories that way. I chug the beer until the bottle is empty and then slam it on the table.

Jake looks up at me with a goofy grin on his face. I glance at his bottle that is still mostly full.

"You're going to have to drink up for what I have planned for you tonight," I say.

His grin wavers just a little. "And what's that?" he says leaning into my ear.

"You'll see," I say with a wink.

I shake my head putting the memory away. That night didn't end in sex like I thought it would. Jake was too much of a gentleman. It's what made me fall for him. Looking at him now I know I have zero chance of getting lucky tonight too. I shouldn't even be thinking about it. I'm here to make him feel better, not hit on him.

Jake finishes about half of his drink before I ask him again, "So, what happened?"

"I don't want to talk about it."

"Yes, you do. You need to talk about it. It's the only way you can move on."

"I didn't have to talk to anyone to move on from you."

I close my eyes as the sting sets. "I'm sorry for everything I put you through. Really, I am."

He takes another sip of his drink but still doesn't say anything. I sigh and take another sip of my own scotch.

He's not going to say anything. He's not going to let me help him. I've hurt him too much.

"Karissa broke it off because she said I work too much. She doesn't want to be married to somebody who doesn't put her first." Jake shakes his glass and watches the ice rattle around in it. "She's wrong."

"Of course she is. I could see yesterday that you put her before your job," I say.

Jake looks from his glass to me. "That's not why she's wrong. She's wrong for saying she broke up with me because I didn't put her before my job. She broke up with me because we were wrong for each other. We have been for a long time."

I take another long sip of my scotch, each sip tasting better than the previous one.

"She broke up with me because she thinks I'm in love with someone else."

I shouldn't ask what I'm about to ask. I shouldn't say anything or do anything when Jake is obviously hurting and obviously getting over a very recent breakup. But I have to know.

I look at my glass, not able to meet his eyes, as I ask, "Is she right? Do you love someone else?"

Jake moves his hand under my chin and forces me to look at him. He forces me to look into his deep eyes as he says, "Yes."

I shouldn't do what I'm about to do. I should give him time to digest what happened. I should give him time to mourn the loss of his relationship. I should give him time to fight for her.

I can't wait though because he could be everything I've been looking for.

My hands go around his neck, and I pull his lips the remaining few inches to mine. I kiss him. And he kisses me back. As soon as his lips touch mine though, I know it is a mistake. The kiss is nice, better than nice. The kiss is great. But I realize, as soon as our lips meet, that neither of us is thinking about the other. He's thinking about *her*. And I'm thinking about *Beast*. I know that this kiss doesn't compare to any kisses that either of us has had in the past.

I slowly remove my lips from his and keep my eyes closed as I whisper, "I'm sorry. I shouldn't have done that."

"Don't be sorry. I want…" He doesn't finish his sentence as his lips are back on mine, attacking me, begging me to make his pain go away.

I give in. I kiss back, hard and fast, trying my best to erase *her* memory from his mind. I bite and nip at his lip, brutally trying to make him focus on me instead of her. I thrust my tongue into his mouth, trying to wipe her away.

It doesn't work. Her memory seeps back, and I can tell by the way he's kissing me that he's not really here; he's still with her.

And I'm still with Beast.

I don't care though. I will let him kiss me for as long as he needs. He deserves that after I broke his heart. He deserves to have the chance to lose himself in me.

I let him continue to kiss me until the kisses change. Once they change to something more aggressive, demanding more than just a kiss, I realize it's time to stop. I push him away, slowly and calmly, so as not to cause him more pain.

"I won't be the woman you fuck tonight to make you forget about her."

Jake nods.

We go back to our respective drinks, trying to comprehend what just happened and what should happen now. Neither of us has an answer, so I order more drinks, like that's the answer. We drink more. We sit in silence longer. We gaze at each other longer, both wanting to find a hotel room to fuck in to wash the others away even though we know we could never be a part of each other's future.

"Do you have a place to stay tonight?" I ask.

"I was just planning on staying at a hotel for tonight, and then I'll start to look for an apartment in the morning." He sighs. "That is, if she won't take me back."

"Do you think there's a chance of that happening?"

He looks at me with such sadness in his eyes. "No. She won't take me back. And I shouldn't want to take her back."

I nod. "You can stay at my place tonight."

"I don't think that's a good idea."

"Sure, it is. I have a spare bedroom. We are both adults and can control ourselves." I smile. *For now*, I add to myself.

Jake nods. "Thank you."

We finish our drinks, and I pay the tab, despite Jake's protests. I text my driver, George, to come pick us up, and then we walk outside the bar into the warm night sky. We have been drinking for hours now, but no matter how long we drank, it didn't wash away his pain, like I'd hoped it would. I can still read his pain all over his face. And there's nothing I can do to help him.

George pulls up in the blacked out sedan, and we silently climb in. George doesn't question which strange man he's driving back to my apartment. He's done it more than enough times to make assumptions about what we're doing. Even though it's not about that.

Jake doesn't say anything to me as we ride back.

George pulls up in front of my apartment twenty minutes later.

"Shit. I forgot to ask if you needed us to stop by your place first, so you could get some things."

Jake shakes his head. "That's not necessary, but thanks."

I frown, but don't push it. If he says he doesn't need anything, he doesn't need anything. We climb out of the car and walk up to the entrance of the massive apartment building. I love this building. It has Old World charm while still having all the best modern conveniences.

Tom, my doorman, holds the door open for us. "Good evening, Miss Scarlett, sir," Tom says to both me and Jake.

"Good evening, Tom," I say, smiling.

Jake barely acknowledges Tom, only nodding his head in Tom's direction before walking past him.

"Thanks, Tom," I say.

In the center of the apartment building, Jake and I walk onto the elevator, and then I press the button to the top floor. I watch Jake out of the corner of my eye and see when he notices that I live on the top of the building, his eyes widening just a little.

Maybe inviting him to my apartment is a bad idea?

I don't want to emasculate him when he sees that my apartment is probably ten times nicer than his. I just want to give him a place to sleep, so he doesn't have to worry about his fiancée.

We step out of the elevator when it stops on the top floor, and I pull my keys out of my purse. I walk to the single door on this floor and put the key inside to unlock it. I push the door open, holding it for Jake, and I flip on the light switch that turns on all the lights in the living area.

When Jake enters, he says, "Holy shit, Scarlett. This place is fucking amazing."

I smile as I look around my apartment. There are floor-to-ceiling windows that cover two stories, making my living space look huge and grand. All of my white-colored furniture helps to make the room seem even that much more spacious. The stainless steel appliances in the kitchen along with the white cabinets and white-colored granite really make the room pop. A spiral staircase in the center of the room, leading up to my bedroom that over-looks the space, finishes what can be seen from the entrance.

"I know. It's pretty great, right? Who would've thought I would build an empire big enough to allow me to afford a place like this on my own? Everybody thought I'd just be living on my parents' money at this point or be married to some rich guy who could afford a place like this."

Jake steps into the center of the room and looks around. "You're wrong, Scarlett. Everybody thought you would have this and that you would get it on your own." He looks at me. "At least, I did."

I suck in a breath at his words. I don't believe him for a second, but it's nice to hear that somebody believed in me, even back then.

"Here, let me show you to your room," I say.

I lead Jake to the one guest room on the main floor. I open the door and click on the lights to the spacious room that contains a king-size bed, a sitting area, a closet, and its own private bath.

"I think this will do just fine," Jake says with a sly smile on his face.

"Good," I say.

I walk back to the living space, and Jake follows. I don't really know what to do at this point. It's about ten o'clock at night, well before my bedtime, but it's not like I can just go upstairs and sleep. It doesn't seem like Jake is ready for sleep either.

"Would you like another drink?"

Jake nods as he makes himself comfortable on the white sectional in my living room. I walk to my bar in my kitchen and pull out the one bottle of scotch I have. I pour a healthy dose of scotch into two glasses. My hand shakes slightly as I pour. Except, when I hand Jake his glass of scotch, that's exactly what the gleam in his eyes says he wants.

And who am I to resist that look?

I take a seat on the sectional, as far away from Jake as I can get, and begin sipping on my scotch. I'm hoping that, if we drink enough, we will each just slip into a coma, so I won't have to tell him no and break his heart again. I'm afraid he thinks the reason I brought him up here was to sleep with him even though I've already told him no. I'm afraid he thinks that he can convince me to change my mind. And maybe he can.

"You really are amazing, Scarlett. You have done so well for yourself. It is just incredible."

"Thank you. You're pretty amazing yourself."

"Not like you," he says.

"You went after your dream, the same as me. It doesn't matter that I make more money."

"You're right. I did. But my dream wasn't just about becoming a financial manager. My dream always included the wife and the kids and the happily ever after. So, I don't quite have my dream yet, unlike you, who has already accomplished everything that you've ever dreamed of having."

I pause. "You think I have everything that I've ever dreamed of?"

"Yes. Don't you? You've built an empire. What's left to do?"

"I want the same things you want. I want to be married, have kids, have the happily ever after."

He narrows his eyes at me. "You said that before. But I didn't really believe you then. Since when did everything change?"

"Since I realized that I was missing something in my life. When I come home, I don't have someone to share my life with. I don't want to have to keep going to bars every night to find a stranger to hook up with. I want more."

Jake studies me, but doesn't move or say anything. He just studies me, like he doesn't believe me.

And maybe he shouldn't when the primary reason I broke up with him was because things were getting too serious. He wanted more, and I didn't.

Could it be that, now, we both want the same thing? Could it be that we are both now single and have a chance to have that with each other?

A slow grin forms on his face. "You know, Scarlett, I can't get my deposit back."

"Your deposit for what?"

"The deposit for my wedding."

"I'm sorry. That sucks. We should plan a big party to have instead of your reception."

He nods. "We could. But I have a better idea."

I look at him, confused, not understanding what he's saying.

"Will you marry me?"

I suck in a breath.

He shouldn't have asked me that. He shouldn't have asked me unless he was completely serious because I already know my answer to that question. I already know what I want. I know that Beast will never give me anything long-term. He won't even agree to more than one fuck at a time. And my only shot at being happy is to settle down and forget about men like him.

So, I simply say, "Yes."

14
———

BEAST

I STRAIGHTEN my tie before I walk into the corporate head-quarters of Fledge Real Estate Group. As much as I hate to admit it to my boss, I love jobs like this. They are why I get up in the morning. Exciting. Thrilling. Controlling. And the day ends in destroying someone else's life.

What's not to love?

I make my way toward the receptionist's desk in the center of the main floor.

"Hello. How may I help you, sir?" the young woman behind the desk says, smiling at me a little too brightly.

I don't bother smiling back as she takes in my perfectly tailored suit that fits me like a glove, showing off the muscles lurking beneath. Her eyes stop when she sees the bulge in my pants, and she brightens, hoping that she will get a chance at seeing my cock in person and not just beneath my pants.

Not a chance.

She's my usual type. Young, blonde, nice rack. But I don't want anyone anytime soon. Not after Beauty destroyed me for any other woman.

"I'm here to see Brett Fledge."

"And your name, sir?"

"Julian Vulture," I say.

She nods as she finds my name on Brett's schedule for the day. "His office is on the six floor. You can take the elevators behind me. I will let the receptionist on his floor know you are on your way up." She hands me a name tag. "Here's a visitor's tag. You can head on up now."

I take the name tag and walk past her desk. Then, I crumple the tag in my hand before letting it drop to the floor. I'm not wearing a damn name tag. I press the elevator button and then climb on. Alone. *Thank fucking God.* I don't want to deal with strangers right now.

I press the button for the sixth floor and then ride in peace as I make my way up to Brett's office. I climb out and am immediately met with another young woman sitting behind a desk.

"Mr. Fledge is in another meeting right now, Mr. Vulture. You can take a seat over there," the woman who isn't as hot as the receptionist downstairs says, pointing to a couch in a small waiting area.

I glare at her. "I don't like waiting."

Her eyes widen in shock. I doubt anyone has ever said that to her before. Brett is always the big dog when people come to visit him here. There is never any worry about making people wait to see him.

"I'm...I'm sorry, sir. I don't..."

I roll my eyes at her blubbering. "It's fine. Just ensure that Brett knows that I don't like waiting."

"Yes, Mr. Vulture. I will let Mr. Fledge know."

I nod and watch her walk back behind her desk. I pull my phone out of my pocket. I ignore the missed messages from my employer and employees, and instead, I go to my guilty pleasure.

I text her.

Me: Your begging won't get you anywhere, Beauty. I'm the one in control. I decide when or if we fuck. I decide how. Your only job is to obey me. But, after I saw you with him, I'm not sure we can ever be together again.

I press Send and then wait. She doesn't answer immediately. I didn't expect her to. But she will eventually. She always does.

"Mr. Vulture, Mr. Fledge can see you now," the woman behind the receptionist desk says.

I get up from the uncomfortable, tiny couch that I know is meant to weaken his adversaries before he lets them into his office. It doesn't work with me.

I follow the woman to the office door that sits just on the other side of her desk, like he needs a guard to watch over and protect him.

The woman knocks on the door and then opens it. "Mr. Vulture, sir."

She holds open the door for me, and I step in. Brett stands from his desk and walks over to me. He extends his hand to me, but I don't take it. He lets it slide back to his side.

"Thanks, Jeannette," Brett says to the woman, who leaves us be.

He motions for me to take a seat in a chair opposite his large wooden desk. I do, and he takes a seat back in his chair behind his desk.

"Your name suits you, Mr. Vulture," Brett says.

I nod. "It does, Brett," I say, letting him know I won't deal with formalities of calling him by his last name.

Brett frowns. "I knew I shouldn't have even taken this meeting."

"You shouldn't have, but you did. So, let me say what I have to say, and then neither of us has to see each other again."

"Fine. Let's hear it."

I smile and pull the paper out of my briefcase. I fling it in front of Brett.

"What's this?" he asks.

"The agreement you are going to sign that will give me control of Fledge Real Estate."

Brett's frown deepens. "Like hell it is!" He tosses the paper back in my face.

I crack my neck back and forth, not the least bit fazed. This is always the initial reaction. Now, it's my job to close. "I would reconsider if I were you."

"Fledge Real Estate is not for sale! I don't know what the hell you are thinking, coming in here and demanding that I sell my company."

I smirk. "That wasn't me *demanding*. It was me *asking*."

"This meeting is through." Brett presses the button on this phone to call Jeannette back in here to escort me out.

Like I said before, *Wuss*. He can't even throw me out of his office on his own.

"We are not finished."

I pull out my phone and find the inappropriate pictures. I smirk as I look at the pictures of Brett—a middle-aged man with a beer belly, tied up, with two women all over him. Brett is supposedly happily married to his wife of fifteen years with two young kids at home.

I slide my phone across his desk. "Look at the pictures."

He does. "You bastard."

I smirk, but don't disagree. I am a bastard. I'm also much worse.

"Now that I have your attention—"

"You can't do this. It's illegal."

"I can do this, and I don't deal with such things as legalities. I take what I want. It's as simple as that."

"What do you want? What do I have to do to keep these pictures from going public?"

I've won, I think. *That was simple.*

I slide the paper he threw at me earlier back across his desk. "You agree to our terms. You will have more than enough money to live off of, and we will get your company."

"Why would you want a real estate company? That's absurd. I shouldn't sell for so little."

I nod. "I think you are forgetting the additional payment of those pictures not being all over the six o'clock news tonight."

Brett's mouth drops. "You wouldn't."

"You have until five p.m. to sign the paper, giving me full ownership of your company. If you don't, those pictures will be all over the six o'clock news."

I reach over the desk and snatch my phone back out of his hands. I pick up my briefcase and exit his office. I dial the number. "It's done."

15

SCARLETT

Fuck! Fuck! Fuck! What the hell did I just do?

I just said I would marry my ex-boyfriend after his fiancée had just broken up with him. I'm not even over Beast yet, and I've already decided on having a future with Jake even though he isn't over his ex.

After I said yes, Jake and I spent the rest of the evening drinking, kissing, and imagining our future lives together. At some point in the night, we drank enough that we both passed out on the couches.

Now, the morning light is streaming in through my windows, and I realize what a stupid fucking mistake it really is.

How could I be so stupid? How could I say yes to marrying someone I hadn't had a relationship with in over ten years?

I get up from the couch, careful not to move too fast, as Jake is still sound asleep on the other half of the sectional. I tiptoe up the stairs to my bedroom and shut the door before taking a sigh of relief. I can't face Jake right now, not until I get my shit figured out.

I walk to my bathroom and flick on the lights before I

head to my shower and turn it on full blast. I quickly strip off my clothes, like stripping it off will erase everything that happened in the last twenty-four hours. I know it won't, but it makes me feel like it could. I quickly step into the shower and immediately feel relief as the hot water pours over me.

I let the water drown out any memories from the last twenty-four hours. I just focus on how the water feels as it pours over my head. Amazing. Refreshing.

When I stand in the shower so long that I don't even remember what got me upset in the first place, I turn the water off. I grab a towel and wrap it around my body before stepping out of my waterfall-like shower that looks more like a cave filled with gorgeous rocks.

The door slamming downstairs though reminds me that Jake is still here. It reminds me that I said yes to a question that I never should've said yes to. Reminds me that I royally and totally fucked up.

I get dressed quickly, putting on a pair of jeans and a tank top, not caring that it's a workday and that I should show up in something a little nicer than jeans. I run a comb through my hair but don't bother blow-drying it, nor do I put on any makeup. I can't remember the last time I went outside without fixing my hair or makeup.

Once dressed, I run downstairs, hoping to solve whatever happened with Jake. To erase what happened last night and blame it on the alcohol we both drank. Blame it on Jake's broken heart. A broken heart that he still has a chance of fixing with Karissa.

But, by the time I get downstairs, Jake is already gone. He didn't leave a note. I check my phone, but there are no new messages from him. He just left, like last night didn't even happen.

Maybe it didn't. Maybe it was all a dream.

I glance at the clock on my phone. It's only six thirty a.m. I still have plenty of time to get ready and make it into work on time. Properly. So, I head back upstairs, change out of my jeans, and put something more appropriate on along with doing my hair and makeup.

And then I head into the office, like last night didn't even happen.

"Glad to see you made it into the office today. I was beginning to think that you decided to take another day off," Preston says.

I roll my eyes at him as I unlock the door to my office. "I'm five minutes late, Preston. I don't think that's enough to worry about me not showing up to work."

"Well, after you were pulled away from work two times now, I wasn't sure if you would show up again this morning. I wasn't sure if you'd be able to face your one-night stand at work."

I pause in my tracks. "Jake is here?"

"Yes," Preston says slowly, like he thinks I'm crazy.

I contemplate on how to handle Jake. I wasn't sure if he would show up to work today between what happened with him and Karissa and what happened between me and him. I thought it would be too much for a man. I guess I was wrong.

"Can you have Jake meet me at his earliest convenience?"

"Sure, just as long as the meeting doesn't end with you running off again and leaving me here to do all your work."

"Relax, I'm not running off again. But, even if I do, you

have been doing a great job, so much so that I might even think about giving you another raise."

"Please don't. I don't need any more responsibilities. I just want to be your assistant."

I sigh and continue to my desk where a mountain of papers and designs are covering it. My phone is flashing the number of messages I've already received. I can understand why Preston can't handle this. *I* can barely handle this.

"Just tell Jake to meet me when he can. I promise, I won't run out early on you today, and if I do, you'll get to leave early, too."

Preston narrows his eyes at me, trying to determine if I'm telling the truth or not. Trying to figure out if he should prepare himself for another afternoon of running the company by himself. I don't think he believes me, but he leaves me alone, so I can get started on the papers in front of me and the messages on my phone.

An hour later though, I hear a knock at the door.

"Come in!" I shout, not bothering to get up, assuming it's Preston.

It's not. At the door stands Jake, looking sexier than ever. He hasn't bothered to shave, so there's a nice amount of stubble covering his neck and chin. His hair is in a less than perfect mess on top of his head. And he's wearing the same suit from yesterday.

"Having second thoughts?" he asks as he shuts the door behind himself.

Yes, I think. That's not what I say though. Instead, I say, "No."

"Good." He walks over to me and grabs my hands. He pulls me into a standing position.

I have no idea what he's doing, so I just go with it. He tucks a strand of loose hair behind my ear and reaches behind my neck, forcing my lips onto his. The kiss is sweet, chaste. There's nothing dangerous about it. Nothing that stirs an inner desire inside me. It's just nice.

When he breaks away, I ask the only question that's on my mind, "Why did you leave this morning then? I thought you had changed your mind."

A smile forms on his lips. "No, I had a few things I needed to take care of. But I meant it when I said that I wanted to marry you. I always have. I've spent my entire morning thinking about you, dreaming about you. Haven't been able to get any work done."

"Me neither," I say even though that's not true.

I've been able to get some work done, and the only reason I couldn't was because I was worried that I'd said yes to a stupid question. Wondering why, when I'd said yes to this good nice man, that I was still thinking about my much more dangerous man. A stranger who wants nothing more than a nice fuck with me, but only on his terms.

"Are you free this evening?" Jake asks.

I force a smile onto my lips. "I usually work till nine or ten. After that, I'm free."

"Good. I'll pick you up from here around nine?"

"Yes. I can't wait."

Jake pulls me into one final kiss before he leaves. The kiss just leaves me feeling even more confused than before. It was nice, but I still want more than nice.

As soon as Jake leaves, I pick up my phone and ask Preston to come in.

He comes in the office almost immediately. "You are not going anywhere."

I shake my head. "What are my plans for lunch today?"

He looks at his phone that holds my schedule for the day. "You don't have a meeting until one thirty p.m."

"Good. Can you see if Kinsley is free to meet me for lunch?"

He frowns. "Sure."

"Thanks."

I think I know why Jake wants to take me out tonight, and it's not something that I can handle without talking it out with my best friend even if I don't usually take her advice. I just need to be reassured that I'm doing the right thing. Because, right now, I'm torn between a dangerous life filled with hot sex that I can never control and might never get again and a nice man, albeit a little boring, who could give me the kids and a happily ever after.

"Wow, I get to see you twice in one week. That's a record, I think," Kinsley says, laughing at her little joke.

I frown. I'm not ready to deal with jokes when I have things a lot more serious on my mind that I have to deal with. Kinsley notices as she takes a seat across from me in the booth at one of our favorite Italian restaurants. I study her stomach as she takes a seat and notice a small bump that's beginning to form. It makes me happy to see her with a baby on the way, and just looking at her reminds me that I could have that, too, if I marry Jake.

"What's wrong?"

I take a deep breath. "I think I'm engaged."

Kinsley raises her eyebrows. "You think?"

I rest my head in my hands, trying to make it all go away. "No, that's not true. I'm engaged. All that's left is the ring that I'm pretty sure he's about to give me tonight."

Kinsley's mouth is open. "How do you get yourself into

these messes? Who's the guy? You've been dating somebody and not telling me? But I thought, just earlier, you were talking about—"

"It's Jake."

"Oh."

"Oh what?"

"Nothing. It's just that I always thought, after you two broke up in college, you would never get back together."

"Me, too. But he sort of just showed back up and asked me to marry him after his fiancée broke up with him."

"Oh."

"I really wish you would stop saying that."

Kinsley's cheeks blush a bright shade of pink. "Sorry. I just don't know what else to say. I'm happy for you. I can't believe you're getting married!"

"See, that's the thing. I'm not sure I'm getting married yet either."

"Then, why did you say yes?"

"It's complicated."

"I think you need to start at the beginning and explain everything."

"Are you ready to order?" our waitress says, interrupting us.

"I'll have the Caesar salad."

"And for you?" the waitress asks, looking at Kinsley.

"I'll just have the salad as well."

I shake my head. There's no way my pregnant best friend is only getting salad for lunch.

"She'll have the lasagna as well," I add.

The waitress nods and hurries away before Kinsley can protest.

"I shouldn't eat the lasagna. I'm already gaining weight a little too fast."

"Nonsense. You're allowed to splurge a little bit now that you're pregnant."

Kinsley smiles. "Now, what's going on?"

"Basically, I want what you have, and Jake is the best option for me to get that."

"But?"

"But there's no spark. I want more than just a nice guy."

Kinsley nods. "Sometimes, it takes a little while to get a spark though."

"Maybe. But what if it never happens?"

"It will. It just sometimes takes a better foundation first before the spark happens."

"I guess. It didn't take long though for the spark to happen with my one-night-stand stranger."

Kinsley shakes her head, like I'm ridiculous. "There is only a spark because of how you met. If you had met like normal people and gotten to know each other first, before you had sex, there wouldn't have been a spark either. The real spark only happens after you get to know someone and find love."

I nod. It makes sense but doesn't fully ease my worries.

"So, what are you going to do?" Kinsley asks.

"I'm going to marry Jake, and I'm gonna forget all about my one-night stand." Even as I say it, I'm not sure I will be able to.

"Good."

Our waitress brings our lunch, and we quickly dive into the deliciousness. About halfway through, Kinsley gets up to use the restroom, and I take a moment to check my phone. I have another text message from Beast.

I want to read it. I want to get the thrill, the rush, that I get every time I do. But if I'm going to marry Jake, I have to delete his number. I have to block his number to keep him from texting me. I'm just about to do it when Kinsley returns.

I glance up and look at a pale Kinsley, who doesn't look very good.

"You okay?" I ask, worried that I'm going to have to take her to a doctor or something.

"Yes. Just being pregnant is no fun. The morning sickness never ends. I told you, I shouldn't have had the lasagna."

She pushes the lasagna away from her, and I laugh. I put my phone back into my purse, forgetting about the reason that I got it out.

"You sure you want to be pregnant soon, just like me?"

I look at Kinsley, who looks a little green and pale, but happy. That's what I want—to be happy, just like her. "Yes, I'm sure."

16

SCARLETT

I HAVE Preston bring me some options of dresses that I can wear on a date tonight. That's the benefit of owning a fashion company. There are always hundreds of new dresses at my disposal to wear anytime I want. And the benefit of still having a model's body type is that I can wear any of the dresses that the models wear, which means I have an endless supply of dresses to choose from. I try on a dozen before I find the dress that's perfect for tonight. It's black with a low V neckline, a large slit up the side, and a fairly exposed back. I fluff my hair and redo my makeup as the clock nears nine o'clock when Jake is supposed to pick me up.

"You need anything else?" Preston asks.

"I don't think so." I shake out the nerves in my shoulders and arms.

Preston walks over to me and grabs ahold of my shoulders, trying to calm me. "You look great, and I think saying yes to a man you're so clearly infatuated with is the right decision."

"Thanks."

"Just make sure he signs a prenup before you marry him."

I roll my eyes. "I don't think that's necessary."

"Oh, it's necessary. And you are making him sign a prenup. You're worth a lot more than he is."

"This isn't about money. I trust him."

"Honey, don't ever trust a man."

I nod although I don't agree.

"You're beautiful," Jake says, staying at the door.

I turn to look at him, and my jaw drops. Jake is standing in the doorway in a full suit, combed hair, and a clean-shaven face. I'm glad I changed.

"Thanks. You're pretty good-looking yourself."

"You ready?"

I nod, unable to say any words. Maybe this is what Kinsley was talking about. Maybe this is the moment the sparks start flying.

Jake walks over to me and holds out his arm, which I immediately take, loving the way my hand feels wrapped around his hard biceps.

"You two have fun now," Preston says.

I shoot a dirty glance at him.

Nerves begin forming in my chest as Jake leads me out of my office. We get stares from several of my employees as we walk. I feel anxiety, knowing that, tomorrow, everyone in this office will know that we are engaged. When that happens, there will be no backing out without completely stomping on his heart again and destroying his image in front of everyone.

I already know what they're thinking. They're thinking that I'm the one who broke up his first engagement. I didn't, but there is no way to remove those thoughts from their heads. It's done. So, now, we have to live with that.

Not that I really care about what they think. All I care about is not hurting Jake and also finding happiness.

To my surprise, when we exit the building, a limo is waiting. Jake really went all out tonight. That makes me even more suspicious, thinking that he is going to propose for real. By the end of the night, there might be a ring on my finger. And, this time, when I say yes, I have to be absolutely sure.

Jake helps me into the limo before climbing in himself. The door shuts, and I glance at him and see him staring at me so intently with a hint of love already in his eyes. That's when I am a hundred percent for sure that saying yes tonight will be the right thing. That's all I want—someone to look at me like they love me. God, it's been so long since anyone has ever looked at me like that—not that I have seen anyone long enough to know the feeling. Kinsley loves me, but she doesn't really count. Not even Preston really looks at me that way. No one-night stand or other ex has ever looked at me that way. Jake's the guy for me.

"So, where are we going?"

"It's a surprise."

I smile. "I like surprises."

"I know."

I lean over and kiss him, giving the kiss everything that I have. And he gives me everything he has in return. It's perfect, almost too perfect, but I push that thought out of my head. Instead, I just enjoy the kiss. Enjoy the thought that, after tonight, I'll get to kiss this man anytime I want. He's mine.

We stop kissing when the limo comes to a stop.

I glance up, and that's when I see we're parked outside my building. "What are we doing here?"

"You'll see."

The driver gets out and opens the door for me. I climb out, followed by Jake. Jake holds his arm out for me again, and I take it. He leads me to the elevator and presses the button for the top floor.

I look at him, confused. *Is he just taking me to my apartment? Maybe he thought I needed a chance to change?*

Although, by what I'm wearing, he should know that I don't need to change.

I don't question him now. I don't want to ruin the surprise.

We step out onto my floor, and I begin to pull my keys out of my purse, assuming that we are going to my apartment. His hand grabs mine at the wrist, stopping me from digging any further into my purse. He shakes his head back and forth.

I stop. "What?"

He just smiles. "This way."

I follow him past the door to my apartment and down to the end of the hallway where there's an emergency exit door.

"We can't go out the door," I say with a worried look on my face. I don't want to actually set the alarm off again. It only happened to me once when I went out to smoke, but man, was it embarrassing. That experience alone got me to quit smoking.

"Sure, we can."

I watch in horror as he puts his hand on the door, and to my surprise, the alarm doesn't go off.

"What did you do?"

He just smiles and grabs ahold of my hand. He pulls me through the door and up the stairs to the rooftop. The rooftop is supposed to be closed. But it's obviously not closed because sitting on the top is one single table with two chairs. At the center is a gorgeous arrangement of red roses.

I look to Jake. "How did you do this?"

He shakes his head. He walks me over to the table and pulls out a chair for me. I take a seat. I can't believe he's done all this.

He takes a seat opposite me. "If I remember correctly, Italian is your favorite," he says.

A waiter appears and places a basket of breadsticks on the table along with a bottle of champagne.

I nod and smile. It is my favorite, and I don't have the heart to tell him that I had Italian earlier today. I watch as Jake pops open the bottle of champagne and pours each of us a glass. He lifts his glass, and I do the same.

"To forever," he says.

"To forever," I repeat as we clink our glasses together. I take a sip of the bubbly liquid. *Perfect.* "This is really nice. Thank you for doing this. I can't remember the last time a guy took me on this nice of a date."

He frowns. "Well, get used to it because I'm going to take you on a lot of dates like this. You deserve it more."

"I'm not sure about that." I take another sip of my drink, trying to distract myself from the thought that I know he's going to propose for real at some point tonight, but it's not something that I want to spend the whole night anxiously thinking about. So, instead, I change the subject. "So, what have you been up to over the last ten years? Give me all the highlights."

He nods. "I graduated with my finance degree but then decided that wasn't what I wanted to do. So, after working for a couple of years in finance, I went back to school with the intention of getting a law degree."

"Really? You have a law degree?"

He laughs. "No."

I quizzically look at him.

"I never finished. Only lasted about a year."

"I'm not sure I believe that. Jake Walton always finishes what he's started. Always. At least the Jake that I knew."

He sits back in his chair. "It was hard to quit. Once I realized it wasn't what I wanted to do and that I was just in it to try to get the degree that I started, I realized it was stupid for me to waste my time and money on something that I didn't love."

"Do you love finance?"

He thinks for a moment. "I didn't at first, but I realize I'm really good at it. That I can make a good living at it. I'm not sure if it's love, but it makes me happy and gives me the freedom to spend my spare time doing things I really love."

"And what do you really love?"

"I love my family. I love spending time with my siblings and their nieces and nephews. I love watching sports. I love just having time to myself to relax."

I nod. Jake hasn't changed much in the ten years that we've been apart.

"What about you? What do you love?"

I think for a minute, not really sure how to answer the question. It's obvious that I love all things about fashion and beauty. I wouldn't have started my own company if I didn't. But I don't want to give such an obvious answer.

"I love spending my time doing something adventurous, something new. Something that really gets my blood pumping. But, most of all, I want to spend my free time starting my own family."

I see the shock that forms over his face at those last words even though I'm pretty sure I told him this last night. Although he might have been too drunk to remember. I don't think he thought that I wanted a family. I think he thought that marrying me would mean giving that part up. But hearing me say the words confirms for him that I really am ready to get married, that I really do want to start a family.

"How soon?" he asks.

He doesn't have to clarify what he means. I already know. *When do I want to start a family?*

I smile. "As soon as possible. I would start tonight, if you would let me."

He spews a little of the champagne out of his mouth. He wasn't expecting me to say that I wanted him to fuck me tonight, to impregnate me, to make me his in every way of the word.

"Do you think that is possible?" I grin as I say the words.

I watch him swallow hard, trying to gather himself.

"I think that can be arranged."

Our first course is brought out and placed on the table. A simple garden salad. We both dig in.

After a few bites, Jake asks, "How many?"

Again, he doesn't have to specify what he means. I already know. *How many children do I want?*

"I've never really thought about it before. As many as we can take care of."

He nods and smiles. "Sounds like a plan to me."

And that's when I realize, that's exactly what we are doing. Planning. It's not something that I particularly enjoy doing. I don't even really do it at work. I don't plan for the future. I make the future be what I want to happen. But I guess that's what being in a relationship with another person is. Planning. Sharing. Compromising.

But I can't believe we are doing it before he's even officially asked me to marry him. It's not something that I thought I would ever do.

"I just need you to answer something for me, Scarlett. What changed? What changed in the last ten years since I knew you? Because the woman I knew before would never have agreed to anything that I'm saying."

I think for a moment, not really sure what to say. I know my answer is important. I know that, if I don't say the exact right words, this might never happen. So, I take my time to say the words, knowing they have been there all along, "Nothing's changed. This is what I've always wanted. I've always wanted a family. I just wasn't ready to have one until now."

A slow smile spreads across Jake's face. He stands up and walks over to my side of the table.

I freeze. *This is it.*

Instead of kneeling down, like I expect him to, his lips crash on mine in a perfect kiss. I kiss him until he controls my whole mind, so all I think about is this kiss. Until all I want is to continue kissing him forever.

He does not continue the kiss that long though. Instead, as he pulls away, with the kiss lingering on my lips, I keep my eyes closed, trying to keep the memory within me.

"Scarlett," he says.

I open my eyes and see him kneeling in front of me. I swallow hard, washing down any nerves that I have.

He grabs ahold of my hand and says, "Scarlett, I know that it's been almost ten years since our last official date. I know that, since then, our lives have taken us on vastly different paths. I know that rebuilding a relationship will be far from easy or quick. But I don't want to wait to start the journey with you. I don't want to wait to make sure that this is the right thing because I already know it's the right thing. Scarlett, will you marry me?"

"Yes."

I watch in amazement as Jake produces a box containing a large oval-shaped engagement ring. It's beautiful, elegant, and simple. I know from the size that it cost a pretty penny. He places the ring on my finger. I can't decide if I should study it more or throw my arms around Jake. So, I do both.

"You like it?"

I release him, so I can look at him. "I love it."

"Good."

Jake begins to go back to his seat, but I'm not done with him yet. I grab the collar of his shirt and pull him to me, devouring him with my lips and tongue.

I need him now. I need him to erase every man from my lips. I need him to erase every man from my body. I need to feel like he is the only man in my life. Because, from this moment on, he is.

He accepts my challenge as his kisses intensify with mine. His hands tangle in my hair as my fingers begin to pull at the buttons on his shirt. I need him undressed, so I can have him right here on the rooftop. I move my kisses from his lips to his smooth neck.

He groans as I do. "Fuck, Scarlett."

His moans and cursing just make me want him that much more. So, instead of unbuttoning his buttons one at a time, I grab each side of his shirt and rip it open. He growls when I do, just like—

I step back and look at Jake.

"What?"

"I have to ask you something."

Jake pants hard as he waits for me to ask the question that I'm not sure I should be asking. If I ask him and I'm wrong, then for no reason, I will have just brought up the fact of how recently I've had sex with someone else. But if I'm right, then all my dreams are about to come true.

I take the chance. "Did you fuck me in a hotel room a couple of days ago? And then again in a restaurant restroom?"

Jake raises his eyebrows in complete shock. A grimace comes over his face. And redness flushes his cheeks.

He's pissed. I was wrong.

"What are you talking about?"

"Nothing. I was wrong. Let's just enjoy the rest of our dinner."

Right on cue, the waiter brings us two giant plates of pasta and sets them on the table with a smile. I smile at the waiter. Jake, on the other hand, doesn't.

He begins pacing back and forth on the rooftop, trying to decide if he should be angry with me or not. I don't feel that there's any reason he should be, but then again, I'm not Jake.

"Let me get this straight. You fucked a man in a hotel room and a restroom, and you thought it was me. How's that possible?"

I sigh, realizing he's not going to let this go without an explanation. "Because it was dark, and he was a stranger. Just now, when you growled, it gave me a flashback to then. So, I thought, maybe it was you."

"So, you just said yes to me even though you let a man fuck you a couple of days ago?"

"Yes."

"I don't understand you! What the hell were you think-ing?" Jake storms back and forth on the rooftop, unable to stand still.

My voice rises. "I was thinking that I would have a good

time since I didn't have a boyfriend or fiancé. And, when you asked me to marry you, I realized that was what I really wanted. You of all people should know that, Mr. My Fiancée Just Broke Up with Me the Same Day I Officially Asked You to Marry Me."

He runs his hand through his hair as he continues to pace, not seeming to listen to any of my words.

"Will you please just sit down and finish our dinner?"

He stops and looks at me, but from the look of pain and anger on his face, I can tell that he can't just sit down. He can't just let this go.

"I can't. I'm sorry." He turns around and walks toward the exit.

I stand from the table, planning on running after him. "Wait!"

Jake turns for just a second. "No. I just need some space."

I freeze in my tracks, a foot away from the table, and I watch the man I just said yes to walk away from me.

How the hell did I fuck this up so much?

I sit back in the chair instead of running after the man who just put a ring on my finger. I hope that, if I stay here long enough, he'll just come back, so we can fix this.

I pull the ring off my finger and stare at it as my own anger boils inside me.

Who is he to get mad at me for sleeping with another man so soon before I said yes to him? Who is he to get mad when he was supposed to marry another woman just a couple of days ago?

I don't deserve this. I deserve better.

I pull out my phone and text.

17

BEAST

I STARE at the woman sitting across the boardroom table from me. She's one of the most ruthless competitors I've ever faced. This job is going to be harder than I thought. Of course, I've done my research on her. She's ruthless, tough, and smart.

Tania Griggs smirks at me with her arms folded across her full chest. She's a good-looking woman, and she knows how to use it to her advantage, especially in a world where she deals mostly with men. That's not going to work with me. Her good looks are not enough to convince me to put my guard down.

"I see that we don't have a deal then," I say.

"You would be right, Mr. Bolt," she says.

"That's too bad," I say, getting up from the table. And it truly is now that I'm going to have to find another way to do my job. I don't accept defeat. If I did, I wouldn't have this job.

Tania stands as well. "I need to speak with Mr. Bolt alone for a moment," she says to the men on either side of her.

They all nod and begin exiting the room. I raise my head toward her.

Maybe I was wrong about her. Maybe she does want to come to a deal.

"Change your mind and don't want your board to know, huh?"

She smiles as she walks around the table toward me. "So sure that you can get me to change my mind? Typical man. No, I have a different proposition for you."

I narrow my eyes and frown, not liking this at all. I don't give up any control unless it's to my benefit, and I know whatever she proposes won't be to my benefit.

"What's the proposition?" I glance at my watch. "I have other places I need to be."

She smiles and adjusts the tie around my neck before letting her hand slide down my hard chest. "I think you and I would make quite a pair. You obviously have a good business sense; otherwise, you wouldn't be after my company. So, how about, instead of trying to steal my company from me, you come work for me? I could use a good partner, and I mean that in more ways than one," she says, winking at me.

I forcefully remove her hands from my chest as I glare at her. "I don't need a partner. I work for myself. And I guarantee, by the end of this week, your company will be mine."

She just laughs. "I don't think so. You don't work for yourself. You have someone you have to answer to, but if you came and worked for me, you wouldn't have anyone to answer to."

"No? I would have to answer to you. And I don't answer to other people. I control my own life. And, like I said before, I want this company, so it will be mine. Simple as that."

She sighs. "Too bad. There were a lot of things I wanted to do with you."

She moves out of my way, and I walk past her. I walk to the elevator, press the button, and then wait. I feel my phone buzz in my pocket, so I pull it out and smile when I see Beauty's name flash across my screen.

I open the message.

Beauty: I shouldn't want you, and I'm not going to have you again, but it doesn't stop me from imagining all of the things that we could do together if we had one more chance. I could suck your cock, take it down my throat. You could take me against a window, so the whole world could see. There's the ocean and the beach. I can only imagine what you could do to me there. In the back of the car or in a dirty alleyway. I can only imagine how good it would feel to have your cock inside me again. I can only imagine because I can't have you again since you won't say yes. That's all you have to do. Say yes, and meet me here at my apartment. I'm sure you already know the address.

My cock instantly hardens at her words. Her words are exactly what I want to put this whole disaster of a day behind me. I need her, and from the sounds of it, she needs me just as much. I begin texting her back.

She said she was at her apartment. Having her there will be easy enough.

My phone buzzes, interrupting my text message.

I growl in frustration but answer anyway, "Yes?" My voice is short and harsh.

"Is it done?"

"Not yet. It will be."

"That's not acceptable. We need it done tonight."

"It will be." I end the call and then delete the message that I started. Beauty will have to wait.

I step into the elevator and contemplate my next move. But I realize there's really only one move.

I step off the elevator and onto the main floor. I dial Tania's number.

To my surprise, she answers on the second ring, "I knew you wouldn't be able to resist calling me. Change your mind so soon?"

"I'm picking you up in thirty minutes."

I can practically hear her smiling on the other end of the phone.

"Thirty minutes is a little early for me. I was thinking more like an hour."

I shake my head even though she can't see me. "Thirty minutes or nothing." I'm tired of playing this woman's game.

"Thirty minutes, it is."

"You're late," I say as I pick Tania up from her office.

She rolls her eyes. "So, where are you taking me, Gerard? I mean, are you simply taking me back to your apartment? Because I'm fine with that. I'm not the type of woman who needs to get to know you first. I know exactly what this is. It's one night to fuck and get our sexual frustrations out of the way, so we can come to an agreement."

I nod. "That's the plan."

I begin walking.

Tania hurries after me. "Are we not going to take a cab?"

"No."

"So, you live close?"

"No."

"So then, what are we doing?"

I ignore the woman and keep walking. She has made today a living hell. And she's the reason I can't go see Beauty right now.

"Gerard, where are we going?"

I freeze at her insistence. I can't take this woman anymore.

I push her into a dark alley. "Right here."

18

SCARLETT

I RUB MY EYES, not caring if I smudge my makeup. I know, from not getting any sleep last night, that I already look like hell. Dark circles have formed under my eyes. My eyes are red, and my body is tired. I'm a mess. And all because of two stupid men.

One man, I thought was a nice guy. He could have been a perfect husband, father, and eventually lover. He's not a nice guy though. He's mad at me for something that he is just as guilty of. I'm an idiot for thinking that we could rush into a relationship and just pick up where we'd left off. There is a reason we broke up in the first place, and this is it.

And another man, I already knew he was a dangerous, dark man. He didn't give a fuck about me. I texted him over and over again last night, but I never got a response. He never came for me.

He's a dick, and Jake's a bastard.

And I'm all alone now. And that's the way I plan on keeping it. I don't need a man. I just need to be alone. I need to work. I need to go back to having fun.

I walk into my office building, more determined than ever to just focus on my work today.

"Congratulations," a woman in accounting says as I walk by.

I smile and nod even though I have no idea what she's congratulating me on. Maybe it has something to do with getting one of the best designers in the business on board. It doesn't seem that weird until I walk past another woman who also congratulates me, followed by another. By the time I make it into my office, I'm thoroughly confused.

I take my desk just as Preston enters my office.

"Congratulations."

I look up at him and frown. "Why is everyone congratulating me?"

He incredulously stares at me. "Funny."

"I'm serious. I have no idea why the whole office is congratulating me."

"Because you said yes to Jake."

I frown. "How does anybody know about that?"

"Because it's office gossip. Jake told one person, and now, everybody in the whole office knows."

"But it's not the truth. I'm not engaged."

"What do you mean, you're not engaged? Jake showed me the ring yesterday. You didn't say yes?"

"No, I did."

Preston laughs. "Honey, if you said yes, that means you're engaged."

"I said yes, but then he stormed off when I told him that I slept with a complete stranger only a couple of days previously. So, that effectively put a kibosh on the whole getting-married thing."

Preston looks at me with confusion on his face. "I think

the two of you need to have a long discussion because I'm pretty sure Jake still thinks you're engaged."

I sigh. I don't want to deal with this. I don't want to deal with him. After the crazy week I've had dealing with two deranged men, I just want to bury myself in my work. "Well, he'll have to wait. I'm sure I have a mountain of paperwork to catch up on, and I know my afternoon is booked solid."

"Maybe this is one of those times when you should cancel your afternoon? I can handle it, I promise."

"No. I want to. And I don't want to deal with Jake right now."

"Are you sure?"

"Yes. And make sure Jake doesn't visit me. If you could help put the kibosh on the rumors about our engagement, that would be helpful."

Preston sighs. "I don't think that's a possibility, but I'll see what I can do."

"Thank you, Preston." I fire up my computer and watch as the emails pour in. I could easily lose myself in the emails for several days, and that's exactly what I plan on doing.

"Can we talk?"

Damn it! I was hoping I could avoid Jake all day, but he's found me.

"No."

Jake slips into my office anyway and shuts the door behind himself.

"I told you, I don't want to talk right now. Have a

meeting in about twenty minutes that I need to prepare for. It'll have to wait."

"I can be fast."

"I don't want to hear it, Jake. Last night was a mistake."

"You're right. Last night was a mistake. But it was *my* mistake, not *yours*. I'm the one who fucked up."

I look up as Jake walks closer. Not knowing what he wants, I glare at him, hoping that he'll go away.

"I'm sorry. I messed up. I shouldn't have gotten mad at you for sleeping with another man when I've been sleeping with another woman for the past few years. It wasn't fair of me. And I regret it. I am a dick."

"*Dick* doesn't even begin to cover it. You're a bastard and a jerk."

He smiles. "Yes, I am all of those things. But I want a chance to prove to you that I can also be better than that. I can also be the man you want to marry."

"Doubtful."

"Just give me a chance. This weekend, let me make it up to you."

"I really think we both just need to give it a rest. Just go back to being friends and see where it leads. I don't want to force this."

"I don't want to force this either. But we're not forcing it if it feels right. Just give me one more chance. I promise, I'll make it right."

"Just like you made it right when you spread the rumors in this office that we were already engaged?"

"As far as I'm concerned, we are. But I will re-propose hundreds of times if I have to. I'll propose every time I mess up. Because you deserve it."

"How about you just don't mess up?"

"I'll work on that."

"Good."

Jake grins. "Still come with me this weekend?"

I sigh, hating that I've already let my plans of keeping men out of my life fall to the wayside. "I'll go with you this weekend. But we are not engaged. And, if you fuck up again, we're going back to just being friends without a shot of being anything more."

"Agreed."

"Now, go. I have a lot of work to do."

Jake nods and leaves without saying another word. Just as he does, my phone buzzes. I look down and see Beast has texted me.

Beast: God, you're so fucking sexy, Beauty. I want to do all of those things to you. I want to come hunt you down and demand you give me all of those things. I'm so sorry I couldn't come to you last night. I worked late and didn't see your message till this morning. I'm ready for you now. Please tell me I'm not too late. Because I don't think I can continue living without knowing what it's like to bury my cock down your throat. Just say yes, and I'll come hunt you down. Just say yes.

Really? How is it that both men can fuck up so easily one second and then both at the same time decide to try to make it up to me in another second?

I really can't deal with both of them right now. So, I'll just deal with them one at a time. I'll deal with Jake first. And then I'll move on to Beast.

I just have a feeling, by the end of this, I'm going to leave with a broken heart and no one but myself to blame.

19

SCARLETT

Early Saturday morning, Jake picks me up in his Honda Civic. He takes my overnight bag from me and puts it in the trunk as I climb into the passenger seat. He didn't tell me where we're going or what we're doing, so I'm just wearing jeans and a T-shirt, but I have plenty of options in my bag, prepared for any situation.

As he climbs in, I don't bother asking where we're going. I already have a pretty good idea. His family lives maybe two to three hours from here. If I had to guess, that's where he's taking me. He already knows that I love his family. I'm guessing he thinks he can just get me around them again to make me realize how much I want him. He's probably right, but I'm not about to admit that to him.

He begins driving in silence, so I flick on the radio, needing some sort of music to drown out the silence.

After a song or two, I say, "It's not going to work, you know. You can't just use your family as a way to try to make me like you again."

"That's not what I'm doing."

"Isn't it?"

"No, it isn't. I just want to take you somewhere I know you will have a good time. Without any pressure and to see what happens."

I yawn and stretch.

Jake reaches into the backseat of his car, pulls up a pillow, and tosses it at me. "Sleep. You're got a two-and-a-half-hour drive to sleep. And you looked like hell yesterday."

"Thanks for the compliment."

"I'm sorry, but you did. I'm guessing it's because you didn't sleep after what I had done."

I frown. I don't like that he thinks the reason I didn't sleep had anything to do with him. "You aren't the only reason I had trouble sleeping. There's a lot going on at work right now, and all this bullshit is just distracting me."

Jake nods. "Just sleep, and you'll feel better."

I don't argue with him anymore because I really do need sleep. I move the pillow off my lap and put it in the corner between the headrest and the window. I recline a little bit until I'm comfortable, and then I close my eyes as I rest my head on the pillow. Sleep overwhelms me quickly.

"I want you, Beauty. I want you on all fours."

I shiver at his words, but do what he said. I move to all fours and arch my back, giving him a good view of my ass. I feel him up behind me, but he doesn't enter me immediately. Instead, his head moves between my legs, and he takes my pussy into his mouth.

"Oh. My. God."

I feel his lips turn up into a smile as I moan. His tongue twirls around my clit with perfect accuracy. He's definitely a skilled man who knows what he's doing. His rough scruff on his face just adds to the friction and makes me go wild with need for him.

I want him. Desperately.

"I'm going to—"

As soon as I say I'm about to come, he instantly stops. I pant hard from getting so close to coming and then having it ripped away from me.

"Please," I beg.

He obliges. I feel him thrust inside me as his balls hit my clit over and over. His hand comes up and finds by breast. It's exactly what I want; it's exactly what I need. He builds me up over and over, each time just stopping short of letting me come.

"Please," I beg again and again.

"Patience, Beauty."

He doesn't relent though. Instead, he builds us up over and over and still denies us each time. I can't take it anymore. I reach my hand down to my clit, intending to make myself come whether he wants me to or not.

When he realizes what I'm doing, he flips me over in one movement and pins my hands high above my head. He is not going to let me come without his permission. He enters me again and begins the slow torture all over again.

"Please, Beast," I beg again.

"Open your eyes."

I do, and I see my Beast standing over me. It's exactly who I thought it was. A tortured man I shouldn't love. That I shouldn't want. A man more dangerous than even I could have imagined.

"Come now, Beauty."

I OPEN my eyes and pant from my intense dream.

"You okay?" Jake asks.

I nod.

"That was some dream you were having. You were panting hard, and every once in a while, you would mumble something about a beast. Didn't make sense to me. Does it to you?"

"No," I lie even though it makes complete sense.

It's just one more reason I should choose Jake over Beast. Jake is safe. Beast is dangerous. But it doesn't keep me from wanting to know if the danger would be worth it.

20

SCARLETT

JAKE'S PARENTS' house is anything but typical. It's beautiful and large, and despite being over fifty years old, it's been completely renovated. His parents live near a large lake in Upstate New York, making it one of the most beautiful and serene houses I've ever been to.

As I climb out of Jake's Civic, all I can think about is how peaceful it is here compared to the city. Even compared to the house I grew up in Las Vegas, it's larger and more serene here. If I didn't love the hustle and bustle of New York City so much, this is where I would choose to live. It's exactly where I'd pick if I needed a break from my life.

It's exactly what I need right now. And Jake knew that.

Jake walks around to the trunk of his car and pulls our bags out. He slings them over his shoulder like they weigh nothing. I smile a little as he does it. It's a good reminder that there are plenty of muscles beneath his polished exterior.

Jake begins walking toward the door of his parents' house and motions with his head for me to follow. I do.

Before he can get to the front door, his mother and

father run out and embrace him in a hug. I smile and take it in. It must be nice to have parents who care about him so much. His mother looks up after she has finished with her hug, and she sees me. Her eyes fill with a warmness that I haven't felt from any mother figure in a long time.

"Scarlett, honey, it's so good to see you again. Thank you for coming to our anniversary party," Evette Walton says.

She walks over with open arms, and I embrace her. I get a deep breath of what smells like brownies mixed with her motherly perfume, something I haven't smelled in a long time, probably since the last time I embraced this woman.

"It's nice to see you, too, Evette," I say.

Larry walks over next and embraces me in a similar hug with stronger arms to hold me tighter. "I see you made it okay."

I nod and smile.

"Well, come in, come in. Jake, you guys can share your bedroom. I have it all made out for you," Evette says.

When a slow grin forms over Jake's face at the thought of sharing a bedroom, I give him a dirty look.

"I'll just show Scarlett to my room then," Jake says, winking at me.

I don't want to share a room with Jake this weekend. Not when I'm so annoyed and angry with him.

"That's fine, dear. You guys have about an hour before guests will begin to arrive for the party. Plenty of time to freshen up," Evette says.

I swear, she winks at her son.

I sigh. I guess I have no say in how this weekend will go if Evette and Jake are already teaming up against me. I'm sure it's only a matter of time before Larry joins. So, I might as well give in to them and just enjoy the weekend.

I follow Jake into the house, and my jaw drops a little.

It's just as beautiful as I remember. I was only here once before. We didn't stay long, just one night, and we didn't share a room then. It was just after we'd started dating, and Jake had had to fly back here for his brother's wedding. I'd decided to come along, needing a break from school.

And that weekend was just as much of a break as this one is going to be.

Still, even though I've been here before, I forgot how warm it felt inside. I forgot how it felt like a home.

I follow Jake up the curved staircase that overlooks the entrance. The hallways are filled with family pictures of him and his brothers and parents. As we climb up the stairs, I stare at the pictures before my eyes, watching as Jake grew from a naked baby into a striking man.

"You coming?" Jake says when he notices that I stopped to stare at a picture of him at college graduation.

It's the Jake that I know best. Young and carefree, but determined. Now, he's grown into quite the accomplishment.

I nod and continue to follow Jake up the stairs. We walk down the hallway, which is filled with more pictures of him and his family, before Jake opens the door to the bedroom that I haven't been in before. His bedroom.

My eyes widen as I look around the room. It still looks like what I would guess his boyhood room looked like. It's like his parents haven't changed the room at all since he lived here. They haven't turned it into a guest bedroom or gym, like most parents would. It's still the same. The only sign that anything has been replaced is a large king-size bed, sitting in the center, instead of what used to be a twin.

Jake places our bags on the floor as he quietly looks at me. He doesn't say a word. He just leaves me be as I begin to inspect every inch of his room. More pictures of him and his brothers sit in the room. Posters of Angelina Jolie plaster his walls.

I smile. "I didn't picture you as an Angelina fan."

Jake smiles and nods, but doesn't say anything. I don't think he wants to distract me from continuing to inspect his room and from him studying me. I walk over to the shelves of old trophy after trophy—from basketball and football sporting events. I run my hand over the cold, dusty metal that contains a lifetime of Jake's boyhood. I pick up a picture frame of Jake with his arm around a girl in a prom dress. I smile, seeing how happy he is to be taking the girl. I imagine, she's a nice girl, unlike me.

I frown and replace the frame back on the shelf where I found it.

"What's wrong?" Jake asked.

"Why me? You should be with a good girl, like the girl in the picture. Not someone like me."

Jake walks over to me and puts his arms around me, pulling me into a tight hug that's so similar to his father's. "You're exactly what I want. Strong, determined, sexy. And you're enough of an adventure to keep me busy and entertained for more than a lifetime."

I don't smile as Jake lets me go, but I don't argue with him either.

I walk to the bed to pick up my bag. "I should get changed if the party starts soon."

Jake nods. "You can have the bathroom, and I'll get changed here. And don't worry about tonight; I'll sleep on the floor. I don't want to rush anything."

I force my face into a tight smile now as I walk to the bathroom that's off of his bedroom. I close the door behind myself. I'm thankful that Jake doesn't want to rush anything, especially when I'm still angry with him.

But maybe that's the problem—that Jake doesn't want to rush things. That he is too nice. Maybe I want him to push me beyond my limits and show me how much he wants me, despite my protests. Maybe I want a little more roughness, a little more mystery, a little bit of not-so nice.

I try to push those thoughts out of my head as I rummage through my bag to find a dress that I packed. I pick the sexiest black dress that I brought and put it on. My boobs look fantastic in this dress, and my legs look long and lean. And, when I put on the black pumps that go with the dress, fix my hair, and apply a little red lipstick, Jake won't be able to resist me.

The question is, do I have the balls to wear this dress in front of his parents, knowing full well that they will know exactly what I'm planning for later?

A wicked grin creeps up my face. Yes, I do.

Maybe twenty minutes later, when I exit the bathroom, Jake is already gone. Probably already downstairs, helping his parents set up for the party.

I walk down the stairs. Maybe, if I get lucky, I'll be able to corner Jake and give him a taste of what I want to do later. Instead, I get lost in the house. Not literally lost, but my mind wanders as I stare at the pictures of the family. As I stare at the furniture that's a little too worn in a house this nice, yet somehow, it works because I know it contains memories of the family enjoying time together. The house is just a little too dusty because they don't bother to hire maids to clean it. I continue to walk around the house, lost in my own thoughts, for I don't know how long, before I hear voices coming from what I remember to be the kitchen.

"Can I do anything to help?" I ask as I enter the kitchen.

Evette looks up from her station at the kitchen and

warmly smiles at me, but it's not her reaction I'm worried about. It's Jake's. He drops the salad bowl he was holding, and I watch as the glass shatters into pieces on the floor, lettuce scattering. His mouth falls open as he looks at me, showing his shock at what I'm wearing.

It takes him a second to regain his composure, and then he raises an eyebrow at me, as if to say, *You sure you're going with that tonight?*

I smile. *I'm sure*, I silently say back.

"Let me help you with that," I say, walking over to Jake.

I get down on the floor to help them pick up the salad and broken glass, giving him a perfect view of my breasts, as he bends down next to me.

"Thanks," he says as we finish cleaning up the kitchen mess he made.

I try to hold back my giggle because I know what the thanks is for, and it's not for helping him clean up the floor. It's for the bulge in his pants that has been forming ever since I walked in the room.

I move my attention from Jake to Evette, now knowing that there's nothing I can do with Jake for several hours. I'm not going to do anything with him at least until his parents' party is well underway, and our services are not needed.

Evette is arranging cookies and brownies. She most likely home-baked the desserts. Another stark difference between her and my mother. My mother would never be caught cooking anything in the kitchen.

I begin helping Evette arrange the dozens of cookies on the fancy silver platters that she has set out.

Larry calls for Jake to help him move some tables outside, and then it's just me and Evette left in the kitchen.

"It's good to see you and Jake back together again."

I try to figure out what to say to this woman without

lying to her. I don't want to lie. Technically, Jake and I aren't together yet. Also, I don't want to tell her I technically accepted his proposal.

"I'm happy to be here," is what I settle on.

The truth is, I am happy to be here. It's nice to have a weekend away from work and to really get a chance to see if Jake and I could ever work.

"I know you and Jake have a lot to figure out. And there are reasons you didn't work out before. I'm sure those reasons made sense then. I'm just not sure they still make sense now. I know you're still trying to figure out what you want, and I understand that, but give him a chance. He's not a bad boy."

"I will," I say honestly. Because that's what I plan to do.

Her last line has me worried though because she's right. Jake's not a bad man. There's not a bad bone in his body. And I'm afraid I need a little bad boy every now and then.

The doorbell rings, and Evette rushes around the kitchen.

"Let me finish. You go see to your guests," I say.

"Are you sure, honey?"

"Yes."

"Thank you," Evette says as she removes her apron, fluffs her hair, and hurries from the kitchen to the front door.

I finish placing the desserts on the trays and then carry them outside to the table set up with the other food. People are already beginning to gather together outside in the backyard. I remember the yard was my favorite thing about the house. It is large, filled with large oak trees that look older than any of us. There are a couple of gazebos on the property, and now, there are dozens of tables for people to grab food or a cocktail from. The only staff I see are a couple of bartenders manning the bar. The rest are just people who love the Waltons and want to help them celebrate.

It's amazing to see the mix of people who have come out to celebrate—young and old, wealthy and not-so-wealthy friends, family, and acquaintances. All the people here fell in love with the Waltons the second they met them. Because they are nice people, people who you want to be around because they remind you of your own home.

I scan the crowd, looking for Jake, and I finally see him talking with what looks to me like old high school buddies. I leave him to it and walk over to the bar where I order a glass of wine.

"You're my kind of girl. Bar's the first place I always stop, too," Larry says as he stands at the bar next to me.

I turn and smile at Larry as he orders a whiskey on the rocks.

"Glad he traded up from Karissa. Those two never made any sense together, if you ask me," Larry says.

"Thanks," I say hesitantly.

I'm not sure if I like the fact that they already like me better than Karissa. They barely know me, and I still believe that Jake deserves better, someone nicer. All I deserve is...

"Let me introduce you to some of my friends," Larry says.

"I'd be happy to meet your friends."

Larry leads me over to a group of older men, and we begin chatting about everything from my job to politics. It's easy to talk to these men. And it helps me get lost in the evening of drinks, good food, and good friends. Even if they aren't my friends.

The only problem is, I've barely spent any time with Jake.

I see him across the backyard, talking with his mother. I give him the most seductive look I can. My eyes scream with need for sex. I bite my lip a little too hard and then seductively run my tongue over my bottom lip. I nod toward the house, telling him to follow me. So, I begin walking toward the house with the intention of going to his bedroom and waiting for him to follow me and be the bad boy who has to be buried inside him.

21

———

BEAST

Fuck. What am I doing here?

That's the question I've asked myself about a dozen times since I followed Scarlett and Jake to his parents' house. Since I threw on a suit and hid among the crowd of people at his parents' crowded anniversary party. Since I was allowed on the property, despite not being on the guest list. The security here is nonexistent. Basically begging me to follow her here and show her how wrong she is to be with him.

Because she is fucking wrong.

I know she shouldn't be with me, but Jake Walton is the absolute worst man for her. He's not strong enough for her. He's far too nice. And he won't challenge her like she needs to be challenged.

Then, why the hell is she here? That's the question that keeps playing in my head now. *Why the hell is she here? Is she really that desperate?*

I don't know, but I'm about to get some answers.

Scarlett makes her way toward the house, and I know it's my only chance to get her alone. I know it's risky. I know that, by following her, I risk her finding out who I am. But I have to go after her. I have to have her. She hasn't answered any of my text messages, and I simply can't wait any longer. Now that I know that she's been with Jake, I want some damn answers.

Scarlett walks into the house, and I walk in just a few seconds behind her. I glance behind me to see if he's following her. He isn't. He's too tied in a conversation with his mother and her friends. It'll be at least a good twenty minutes before he can get away. More than enough time to do what I need to do.

I follow Scarlett as she slinks through the house to the stairway and goes up the stairs. I wait until she's made it all the way up the stairs and into his bedroom before I follow. I run up the stairs, taking them two at a time, anxious to get to her.

I pause for a second at the door.

Here's where everything could go wrong. If she sees me before I have a chance to turn the light into darkness, then I'll be fucked. Whatever the hell this is will be over. But if I don't open the damn door, I won't get to fuck her.

It's really not a decision.

I push the door open and am happy to see the lights are still off.

"I wasn't sure if you would come," she says.

Her dress is already off and lying on the floor. She's completely naked, standing in his bedroom in almost complete darkness, just a few beams of light sneaking in through the blinds. The light is enough that I know she'll see me if I move toward her even one step. So, instead, I wait for her to come to me, just like I imagine that damn fucker would do.

She takes my bait and walks toward me where I wait in

the darkness, her curves swinging back and forth in the few beams of light that are slipping through the blinds. My mouth runs dry as I watch her, and it's a good thing because it prevents me from speaking even though I want to.

I want to demand her to turn around and show me that tight ass that I fell in love with last time. I want to control her and tell her to get on her knees and suck my cock, like she promised in her text. I want to control her, but I can't. Not until I have my lips on her. Because, when she realizes that it's me and not him, she will have a chance to say no. But as soon as I have my lips and my hands on her, I know she won't be able to resist.

She walks closer and closer until she's just an arm's length away from me. I reach out then, unable to wait any longer, and I pull her fully into the darkness. She lets out a quiet whimper as her body becomes pressed against my chest. I wish I'd thought to remove my clothes while waiting for her to come to me because, right now, I need her skin against my skin.

Our hands grab ahold of each other as our lips find each other again, our tongues tangling together. I feel a desperation oozing from her that I haven't felt before. A desperation for her to get exactly what she's been missing these past few days without me. Something that I know he hasn't been giving to her. She wants to be controlled. She wants to feel that rush of adrenaline. She wants me. And I'm more than happy to give her that.

Kisses tangle together until I have no idea how many times we've kissed. Hands tangle together in hair and clothes. Our bodies cling together, fighting to become one again, if only for a few moments.

Goddamn, she is worth the risk.

Her hands move inside the collar of my shirt, trying to

get at my skin. I love her hands there, but I want her on her knees more. I want to see her gorgeous big eyes looking up at me as she takes my cock in her mouth. I want to see her expert tongue moving around me before I reward her by taking her against the window of his bedroom, so if anyone looked up, they could see an outline of a woman being fucked.

"On your knees," I say.

She freezes, and I think it's because she wants to tell me that she wants to be in control this time, just like some of her text indicated. I can't let that happen now, not when she's been with him. I need to be in control now.

She pushes her hands against my chest and takes a quick step backward and then another. "Beast?"

I take a step forward, but stop short of letting myself into the light. I thought, once I kissed her, she would forget that she came here to fuck Jake instead of me. I was wrong. But there's no point in denying that now that she knows it's not Jake.

"Yes."

"I need you to leave," she says.

She gathers up her dress and slips it back on before I have a chance to capture the image of her naked body in my head forever.

"No."

She shakes her head at me with anger on her face. Her nostrils are flared, her cheeks are bright red, and her hair is a mess on top of her head. And, God, I've never wanted to fuck her more than I do right now.

"You need to leave. Now."

"No. I need to talk to you. Now."

She takes a step forward, and I take a step back, afraid that she might see me.

"You. Need. To. Leave. Now."

"That's not happening. Not until I have you first."

She huffs. "Why are you both such complete idiots?" she says mostly to herself as she runs her hand through her hair. She walks back and forth in the room. "I don't want you. We're through. I'm with Jake now."

Anger boils inside me at the thought of them being together. Really, at the thought of her being with any man other than me. "He's not good enough for you. You shouldn't be with him."

"Then, whom should I be with?" she challenges.

I want to say *me*, but I don't because she deserves better than me. My silence gives her, her answer.

"Because it sure as hell isn't you," she spits at me.

"Anybody but him."

"You don't get to tell me what to do."

"I have before."

"Yeah, well, that's over."

I sigh, hating her words. They are the worst words I've ever heard.

But I have no idea what I have to do to convince her that, at this moment, I would do almost anything. I don't care about my job. I don't care about my life, outside of this room. All I care about is her and having her and wanting her to want me back.

It doesn't make sense. I've never wanted a woman to want me before. I prefer to just control them and tell them what they want, and they almost always seem to oblige. Beauty though, she's different. I love the challenge and her defiance.

"You should go," she says again—this time, her voice soft and defeated.

"No."

"Jake will be here any minute. You should go before he throws you out of the party."

"I don't think Jake's coming."

Scarlett doesn't argue that fact though because she knows, deep down, that he isn't coming. But she will say anything to get me to leave, and I know she doesn't have the willpower to leave me on her own.

"What do I have to do to have you again?"

She just shakes her head and ignores me.

"Answer me," I say, more commanding.

"You can start with showing me who you are."

I don't know why, but I wasn't expecting her to say that. I thought she liked the mystery and not knowing who I was. I thought that was part of the excitement for her.

"Why?"

"Because maybe I would like a relationship with you beyond text messages and you randomly showing up whenever the fuck you want to fuck me and nothing more. Maybe I want to date and see where it goes."

"I don't date. And fucking is as far as this goes."

"Then, show me who you are. Show me why this is as far as we go."

It's what I want, too. God, I want to be able to fuck her in the light of day instead of the darkness. For once, I want to hear her say my name. I want to gain her trust completely. But I know, as soon as she sees me, she'll be gone.

She waits for a moment longer to see if I answer, and when I don't, she walks past me, leaving me alone in the room. In the darkness. Leaving me alone with the one request I can never answer.

Who am I?

22

———

SCARLETT

I SLAM the door shut to Jake's bedroom, and then I begin running down the stairs, trying to get as far away from the bastard as I possibly can. Trying to erase his kiss from my lips. Trying to forget about the fact that I kissed Beast again when I swore I wouldn't. I swore I wanted Jake, not Beast. And I know that, on some level, when he walked in the door, it wasn't Jake, and still, I kissed him anyway.

What is wrong with me? Why can't I let that one night go? Why am I okay with settling for nice? Why am I okay with either one?

Because I'm tired of being *alone*.

I continue walking toward the back of the house, intending to go back outside and enjoy the party, like nothing just happened. I can't though. For one, I look like I just had sex. My cheeks are flushed, my hair is unkempt, and my lipstick is smeared. I would feel too guilty, walking around like that with these people. Too guilty to face Jake right now. I don't exactly have any other place to go though.

I stand at the door that leads back outside to the party, trying to figure out where I could go. The lake is just down the hill from the house. If I could just make my way down there before anyone spotted me, there would be far less people for me to deal with.

I open the door and scan the crowd for Jake. I see him, still in deep conversation with his mother and her friends. So, instead of going left toward him, I go right. I skirt the edge of the party, smiling politely when anyone notices me, but I make my way down to the lake, only stopping once to grab two gin and tonics to take with me down to the water's edge.

I make it to the edge of the water just as the sun is setting over the lake. I hike my dress up and remove my heels before I take a seat on the sand and stick my feet into the lake water. I don't care that the dress is now ruined. All I care about is drinking on the edge of the water, alone, so I can figure out what the hell I'm going to do with the two men in my life.

First though, I down the first gin and tonic and mix that cup with the still full cup. And then I just stare at the sun setting, trying to forget what just happened.

The sun goes down quickly though, and then I'm left in the darkness with only the light from the moon and the flicking of lights from the party behind me. Without those lights, I'd be sitting in the darkness. Just like Beast.

I feel a tear trickling down my cheek. I let it fall. I let myself feel the pain. Even though I don't know why I'm crying.

Beast.

My dark stranger.

My lover.

I didn't realize how much I cared about Beast. How much I wanted there to be a chance of *more* with him. From the first moment I met him in the hotel room, it wasn't just one night for me. My heart has been begging for more and more and more. Never going to be satisfied until I at least get a chance to be with him. But, after tonight, I know that there isn't going to be a chance.

Beast isn't a *more* kind of guy. His secrets are more important than giving us a chance together.

Maybe tonight was for the best. Because, tonight, I can finally let him go, knowing that we will never have a shot.

So, that's why I let the tears that I almost never let out fall. I don't remember ever crying like this, except for ten years ago when I was told that Kinsley was dead. After that, it was only tears of happiness when I found out she was alive. After that, I haven't cried for myself because I have never gone through anything nearly as painful as she has.

Right now, I let myself cry. And cry and cry. Because my heart is broken.

I realize now that, when I said yes to Beast, I gave him half of my heart. And, when I said yes to Jake, I gave him the other half. And, now, I have nothing left.

But maybe Beast confirming that there can't be anything more set half of my heart free? Maybe, once the tears are gone, I can reclaim that half of my heart and decide if I want to keep it for myself or give the rest of it to Jake?

I wipe the tears from my eyes and try to forget about Beast. It should be easy to forget about somebody I didn't even know. I didn't know his name, the shade of his eyes, or what he did for a living. I didn't know any of the important things about him. All I know is that he likes control, he has intensity in his eyes, and he seems to know me better than I know myself. If only he were able to share something with me, anything, show me some sign that he wanted to do more than just fuck me, then maybe he would've been enough. But he's not enough.

I take another sip of my drink as my thoughts turn from Beast to Jake. Jake's caring, nice, a good man. He's everything I should want in a husband and father to any of my children. The only problem is, he doesn't get my heart pumping. And he takes things far too slow. He hasn't even tried to have sex with me yet. Not really. Even when I try, he doesn't seem to want to push forward. Even though we've had sex in the past, albeit it was ten years ago.

I could just forget both men. I could adopt or try surrogacy and have kids by myself. I could do it. Then, I could have the family without having to deal with either of the two men. Or any other man. I could have my own family, and then I wouldn't be alone again.

"Hey, stranger. Is this seat taken?" Jake says as he walks up behind me.

I wipe my face again, making sure all the tears are gone. I slightly turn my head so that I can see Jake. "It's all yours."

I watch as Jake sits beside me on the wet sand. He kicks off his shoes and rolls up his pants legs before sticking his feet into the water.

"Here, I thought you could use another drink." He hands me another gin and tonic, and I take it from him.

"Thanks," I say, smiling at the drink.

Jake even remembers my drink order.

Why the hell don't I see that he's clearly the best choice?

"Sorry I didn't spend much time with you at the party. I thought it was best to give you some space," Jake says.

"I understand. I'm still trying to figure out a few things myself."

"Like whether you want to wear this ring again?" Jake holds up the ring he proposed to me with.

I nod, surprised to see the ring in his hand. I try to think back to where I put it. I remember packing it in my things, but I don't remember taking it out.

"Did you go through my things?"

Jake nods. "I thought you might have had the ring. I thought that, if I could just find the most opportune moment to give it to you again, this time, you would say yes, and it would stick."

I take the ring from his hand and hold it in mine, staring at the sparkly diamond. "And you think now is the most opportune time for me to say yes?"

Jake frowns. "No. I just realized, I don't want to trick you or trap you into marrying me. I want you to want to say yes, no matter if I asked you to marry me in the nicest restaurant in New York City or in front of the city dump. Or after I blurted it out after a night of heated passion. Or while sitting on the edge of the lake in my parents' backyard. I want you to want to say yes because you love me and want to marry me, not because you just want to get married, period."

I take a deep breath in. And then I hand him the ring back. "I want that, too. I'm not able to say that yet. I can't give you a definite yes. I can't give you that. So, hold on to this until it doesn't matter when or how you ask me, until you know I won't be able to help but say yes because I'm desperately in love with you. Not in love with the idea of marriage."

Jake's frown deepens as he takes the ring back and tucks it back into his pocket. "So, where do we go from here?"

"You ask me out. I already know my answer to that question. And it doesn't matter how you ask me; my answer would still be the same. No matter if you asked me in the fanciest restaurant or next to the city dump or while sitting on the edge of the lake in your parents' backyard, I already know my answer to that question."

Jake's grin is larger than I've seen it in a long time, and his smile actually reaches his eyes. "Scarlett, will you go out with me?"

I smile and give him a shot at the other half of my heart that I just reclaimed. "Yes."

I reach my hand to the base of his neck and pull him into a kiss. It's a tentative kiss on both of our parts. He's trying to figure out exactly where he stands, and I'm trying not to compare it to the kiss I had earlier today that wasn't from him. Still, the kiss is nice and exactly what we both need at the moment.

We pull away at the same time—both keeping our eyes closed, both still holding on to each other, just no longer kissing.

"Let's go to bed," I say.

I hear him swallow nervously.

I know the right place to have sex again for the first time in ten years is not in his parents' house, so I put his nerves at ease. "Just to sleep. I'm exhausted."

"I don't have to sleep on the floor?"

I let out a small giggle. "No."

23

———

BEAST

I DRIVE FAST, needing to get somewhere so that I can get a release soon since she wouldn't give me what I needed. I don't understand why I feel like this. And why I won't just go out and pick up another woman. That's the simple solution. Find a new woman. Fuck her. And then get back to my job.

It's not that simple though. My cock doesn't get excited anymore whenever I see any other woman. I don't dream or fantasize about other women, just *her*. I can't do my job properly because, even when I'm in the middle of doing the job, I'm thinking about her.

My mind is a mess, but I'm afraid my heart might be worse. Because my mind can be controlled. I can tell my mind over and over again that she's not worth it. I can remind my mind that being with her would effectively destroy my life. Because that's what I'd be doing—killing us both. My mind isn't the problem.

My heart though...that's another story. I don't understand what my heart is feeling. I don't understand how my heartbeat speeds up when I'm around her. I don't understand why my heart begs me to tell her my name. I don't understand how my heart expects me to give up everything for her. That's something that I have no idea how to control.

I drive faster and faster in my black Mercedes-Benz that has blacked out windows so that nobody can see who I am. Nobody knows who I am. Not her. Not my employers. Not my employees. Not my friends. Not even my family. Nobody knows who I really am and what I really want.

And the only person that I want to know who I really am is Scarlett.

I almost miss my turn because I'm already distracted again, thinking about her. I turn sharply at the last minute and listen to my tires squeal. I swerve into a parking spot before killing the engine and climbing out. Every time I put a step on the ground as I make my way to the building, I take a deep breath, trying to calm myself. It's no use.

I'm still thinking about her with every step. I'm thinking about her plump red lips. Her long mane of hair. Her legs that go on for miles. I think about the strong woman who controls her own empire, who controls her destiny. But, for some reason, she gives the control to me every time I fuck her. I have a feeling she would give more control to me if I would just tell her who I was.

I make it to the door and swing it open as my breathing has now turned into hard pants instead of calming breaths, like I intended. I feel sweat forming on my forehead, threatening to move and sting my eyes. I wipe it off as I walk to the man behind the desk.

"You okay, man? You don't look so good," he says.

I glare at him. "I'm fine. I need an hour." I pull out my wallet and throw some cash on the table.

The man wearing the name tag that says, *Jimmy*, nods and takes my cash. I walk to the shooting range behind him.

I don't bother with the stupid safety goggles or ear protection. I don't have to bother stopping in a locker to get a gun, like most people would. My gun is always on me. I pull my pistol from the back of my pants along with the ammunition I always carry.

I straighten my arms and fire over and over and over at the target of a man across from me. I perfectly hit the target in the head every time. I move my aim from the head to the heart and fire another dozen shots. Each shot perfectly pierces the heart. I continue doing this for an hour until that hour turns into another hour and then another. Until I have no idea how long I've been here.

But it does give me the release I've been needing all day. It gives me the control when I have none over my life. When I've finally had enough, I begin putting the gun and remaining ammunition away into the back of my pants.

"I could watch you shoot all day. I've never seen a man shoot with such accuracy. I know you're not a cop or a military guy. And I know you don't work for any faction of the US government," Jimmy says from behind me.

I turn and look at the older man who runs the range. I haven't ever been to this shooting range before, and for this very reason, I tend not to go back to ranges more than once. I don't want the employees to get to know me. I don't want them to know my story. But no one's ever questioned me before because I only come once and then never return.

"And why do you say that?"

The old man smiles at me. "Because you're the best shot I've ever seen. And no training from any government facility would make you that good."

"I didn't train at a government facility, but that doesn't mean I don't work for the government now."

"Whatever you say. I don't care whom you work for. I

just wanted to let you know that you're welcome back anytime you want, no questions asked. You don't have to worry about hiding who you truly are. I respect you for whatever you are."

I nod, but don't bother saying thank you. "See you around, Jimmy," I say. I walk out of the building and back to my car. I don't intend on coming back again. It's too risky.

I start the ignition in my car and then drive quickly out of the parking lot. I glance at the clock in my car. I was there for almost four hours. Enough time to give me plenty of perspective on my current situation. I can't have her, but the only way I'll be able to let her go is if I find somebody that should be with her. Someone who can take care of her and cherish her in the way that she should be cherished.

I'm not convinced Jake Walton is that man yet. Maybe, after I meet him in person, I'll change my mind. I just need to arrange the meeting.

I dial the number, and the phone connects to my car speakers as I wait for him to answer, so I can schedule the meeting.

24

SCARLETT

When I head back into my office on Monday morning, I feel refreshed. I feel *over* whatever the hell happened between me and Beast. And I feel ready to give Jake the real shot that he deserves. But, most importantly, I'm ready to get back to work and my normal life.

"Good morning, Preston," I say happily as I walk into the office where Preston's already waiting for me.

"Good morning," he says back. "Somebody's in a happy mood today."

"Yep. I had a good weekend, and it gave me some perspective on my life. I'm excited to get back to work today."

"Good, because we have a lot of fucking work to do."

I walk over to my desk and take a sip of my latte that Preston always makes me every morning. "Where do we start?"

Preston smiles, happy that I'm more focused on my work than I've been in a long time. "We start with picking the models you want to use for our national makeup campaign."

I smile. Being a former model myself, it's one of my favorite parts of the job. Picking models to represent my brand. Making girls' dreams come true because that's what I'm doing when I pick a model. I never pick someone who has tons of experience or an actress who wants to make an extra buck by modeling. I always pick somebody new and fresh and give them a new chance at their dream.

"Let's go then," I say.

Preston nods and begins walking to our offices on the main floor where we interview models and do some test shots.

By the time we get there, Jamie, my casting director in charge of finding our models, has already begun explaining to the models how the process works and getting everything organized. She's the best at what she does, and she is one of the most organized people I know. It's why I love her.

"Are you ready to start?" I ask Jamie.

Preston and I take our seats behind the long table that serves as a desk for the three of us while we do the interviews.

"Of course. It's eight o'clock, and we always start on time," Jamie says.

"Good, because we have a full schedule today," Preston says.

"When do you not?" Jamie asks.

Preston just shrugs. "Never."

"All right, we need models one through five," Jamie says.

The models begin lining up on the makeshift catwalk, and Jamie takes a seat next to us. I glance down at the five models' headshots, each one of them gorgeous in their own right. Each one of them would probably do a great job in working for us. But we only need one out of the more than a hundred who showed up today for the job. Jamie tells them to start walking, and they do, one at a time, down the catwalk.

I smile and watch as each of them walks. A couple of them shake a little as they walk, most likely from nerves. One even stumbles in the heels she is wearing. Only two of the first five look confident. I focus in on those two as they walk. Either one of them would do. But I also know from experience that there will be a couple of confident ones in almost every bunch. And those are the ones that I'll have to choose from. We don't have time to train someone who isn't ready yet.

When they finish walking, we ask them to line up. Then, we begin asking them basic questions to see how they do with talking and interacting with the camera since that will be a part of the job while shooting a commercial.

"Why do you want this job?" I ask.

We get the standard answers from most of the girls.

"I've always dreamed of being a model."

"Your makeup line is my favorite."

"You're such an inspiration, and I'd love to learn more from you."

And then one stands out from an unexpected girl. The one who tripped and almost fell. The one who I almost immediately counted out. "Because I'm the fucking right person for this job. I'll work harder than anyone else. And I want to be the next Scarlett Bell. And I will be whether or not I get this chance."

I jot down a note on her headshot. Number three. Emmy Bitton. I know without looking at any of the other women that she will be the one I choose. That Preston and Jamie will fight me on it, claiming that another one was better, stronger, more confident. A better fit for the job. That's not what I look for when I look at models. I look first to see if they are a star in the making. I look for someone like me or someone like my best friend, Kinsley. I look for someone who will change the world, and I know that Emmy Bitton will. And it's not because she just told me that she would. Saying that you're going to do something is just the first part. The actual following it up, that's the key to actually getting what you want and actually changing the world. I have every faith that Emmy will do it even if I don't give her this chance.

We spend the next hour and a half going through model after model, and just like I expected, Preston and Jamie both like another one.

"It's got to be number twenty-five. She was, by far, the best. She has the best face for beauty and more confidence than even you, Scarlett," Jamie says.

"No, no! It's got to be number seventy-two. Did you see how she handled that walk? Flawless," Preston says.

I watch them bicker back and forth, not really adding anything because I already know who we are going to choose.

"What do you think, Scarlett?" Jamie asks. "Number twenty-five or seventy-two? Or did you have someone else in mind?"

"Number three."

I watch as Jamie and Preston dig through their files and notes, trying to find the girl I'm talking about. I hand them my headshot of the girl to refresh their memories. It's easy for me to find because she's the only girl in my Yes pile.

"She's pretty enough, I guess," Preston says. He looks at the picture of the blonde woman who wore her hair in long curls, reminding me of how Kinsley used to wear hers when she was a model. "But she has that small scar on her cheek that will be hard to cover with makeup. And didn't she stumble? I think you got the wrong girl, Scarlett. She's not confident enough."

I point to the girl. "She's our girl," I say.

Preston and Jamie frown at me at the same time.

"Are you sure?" Jamie asks.

"I'm sure."

"I'll make it happen then," Jamie says, standing from the desk and gathering her things to make the call that will change this woman's life forever.

I gather up my things, and Preston and I both walk back to my office. We make it back upstairs when I see Jake standing in my doorway, his arms folded across his chest, with a dumb-looking grin on his face when he sees me.

"So much for getting work done today," Preston whispers in my ear.

I laugh at Preston. "We'll get plenty of work done today. I'm sure Jake just wants to say hi."

But I glance over at Preston, who's eyeing me suspiciously, not believing a word I'm saying. Maybe I'm wrong. Maybe Jake isn't here just to say hi. Maybe he does want to steal me away today and play hooky. Maybe he does want to show me a wilder side.

Jake automatically kisses me when I get close enough to him. I frown, not liking that his kisses are automatic already.

"What's up?"

"I just came to see how you were doing today. I missed you."

"We just got back last night and slept over at my apartment again. I don't know how you can miss me," I say, laughing.

"I'm not sure either, but I do." Jake's large smile returns to his face. "So, do you have any lunch plans or evening plans? Because I don't know how I'm gonna make it through the day if I don't know when I'll get to see you next."

I glance over at Preston, and he's rolling his eyes at Jake's cheesy words.

I want to go out to lunch with Jake, but I can't. I know I already have plans. "Can't do lunch. Already have a meeting lined up. But how about drinks with me and Preston and Preston's new girlfriend?"

I glance over at Preston, who nods like that can be arranged.

"Sounds good to me. As long as I can see my favorite girl, I'll be a happy man."

"Preston will let you know the time and place to meet us."

Jake wraps his arm around my waist and pulls me to him into a kiss, this one more passionate than the first.

"I would say, get a room, but you two might actually do that, and then I'd be left to make all the decisions—*again*," Preston says.

We both pull away.

"I'd better get back to work. My boss is quite the tyrant," I say jokingly.

"I'd better get back to work, too. I wouldn't want my boss to think I was lazy or anything," Jake says.

Jake leaves and heads back to his office, leaving me and Preston alone.

"Funny, I'm not your boss, just your assistant," Preston says.

"You could've fooled me," I say.

Preston shakes his head. "Just get to work before I fire you," he says with a smile on his face.

I finish sending my last email of the day and then holler to Preston, who is sitting in his office, just around the corner from me, "I think it's time to call it a day."

A few minutes later, Preston walks into my office. "Sounds good. My girlfriend, Kathy, said she could meet us there in a half hour."

"Good. I can't wait to meet this girl. And Jake?"

Preston frowns. "Sorry, forgot to tell you that Jake had to cancel. Said he had a late meeting and that he would meet you back at your apartment later."

I frown. I didn't think Jake would work harder than I did. I guess I was wrong. I guess I'll have to wait to see Jake later.

"Let's go then," I say.

Preston nods, and we head out of Beautifully Bell Enterprises to my waiting driver, George.

"How are you doing this evening?" George asks as we climb into the car.

"Pretty good. My date canceled on me tonight, so I am playing third wheel with Preston and his girlfriend."

George raises his eyebrows. "You have a girlfriend?"

Preston rolls his eyes. "Why does everyone keep asking me that?"

George and I both laugh.

George says, "Sorry. I guess I thought that—"

"Yeah, I know. You thought I was gay," Preston says.

"No. I thought that you were a mama's boy and a workaholic, so you wouldn't have time for anyone but yourself," George says.

Preston's phone rings, and he answers it, confirming George's statement that he is a workaholic.

I glance at my own phone and frown because I haven't gotten any text messages from Jake or from Beast. I don't know which one stings more. I thought Jake would text me that he was sorry he couldn't come. I hoped that Beast would have changed his mind and said that he was ready to tell me who he was. That I was worth risking whatever he'd be risking by telling me who he was.

George stops the car in front of a new bar that Preston wanted to try out. We both climb out and walk into the bar. We find a small booth table while we wait for his girlfriend to arrive. The waiter comes over and asks for our drinks. We each order a gin and tonic.

"So, when is Kathy supposed to get here?" I sip on the gin and tonic the waiter just brought us.

Preston nervously glances down at his phone. "She's not coming out."

"What? Why?"

"Work."

"And I thought we were the workaholics. Who'd have thought our significant others would be working harder than us?"

Preston shakes his head and takes a drink. "Good thing we have each other when our significant others don't work out."

I nod. "So, what do you think about Jake?"

Preston stares down at his drink, like it's the most inter-esting thing in the world.

"What is it?" I ask.

"Nothing. I just always pictured you with somebody who was more your equal."

"How is Jake not my equal?"

"I don't know, Scarlett. He's just not."

I swirl the ice around in my drink, but I know exactly what he is talking about. Jake isn't my equal. Opposite maybe but not equal.

But don't they say that opposites attract?

"So, is Kathy your equal?"

Preston shrugs. "No, but she's fun to fuck."

I laugh and spew some of my drink at that. *Who knew Preston had it in him?* "You're such a man, Preston."

He nods.

I glance around the bar that is getting busier by the second. The bar is almost completely full of men.

"If I weren't dating Jake, there'd be plenty of men for me to choose from here," I say.

Preston nods. "It is quite a hopping bar."

Just as he finishes speaking, loud music comes on, and barely dressed men begin dancing as the crowd squeals and shouts in excitement.

"Oh my God, Preston. It's a gay bar."

"It is not," Preston says. But then he laughs when he realizes it's true. "Sorry."

"Don't be sorry." I enjoy the view of half-naked men.

"Come on, let's get you home before you turn a gay man straight," Preston says.

"Hello?" I shout into my apartment as I open the door.

I don't get an answer. I walk into the living room and

flick on the lights. I smile when I see a half-naked Jake passed out on the couch.

I bite my lip as I study his hard, muscular chest that I swear has gotten even more muscular since college. He always did have a good body. I walk over to him, still staring and not ashamed to admit it.

"Jake," I whisper.

He doesn't wake.

I try again, "Jake."

Nothing.

I sigh. If he stays like that on the couch, he's going to have a wicked crick in his neck in the morning. And I can't really resist his half-naked body at the moment. I bite my lip, considering what I'm going to do, but I already know.

I kneel on the floor next to the couch as my lips move to his hard chest. I start at the top, on his hard pecs, kissing each part of his smooth muscles and each crevice between his abs. I kiss softly at first, trying not to disturb him so that I can just enjoy his body.

But then my kisses become harsher and more aggressive, trying to wake him. Trying to get him to want me. To fuck me.

He moans softly as I begin kissing lower and lower on his stomach, but he doesn't wake up. A devious thought creeps into my mind. I know he wants to take this slow, but the speed we are going is ridiculous. And I can't wait much longer.

He's wearing athletic shorts, and I begin pulling gently at the waistband. He still doesn't wake. I pull harder until his shorts and underwear are pulled down, and his cock springs free.

I bite my lip again, staring at it. I thought, by now, he would have woken up.

Do I really have the balls to do what I'm about to do?

Yes.

I move my lips to his cock and began sucking. He moans as I do, but that still doesn't fully wake him up. So, I suck more, harder, faster. I love having his cock between my lips. I love that I can bring him pleasure, even in his sleep. I move my hand to his shaft and begin pumping up and down in rhythm with my lips.

His moans intensify until I'm sure he's about to come, but then he says, "Karissa."

I freeze, not sure what to do. He said her name, not mine. I know he's asleep, and I shouldn't hold him accountable for anything he's said, but it still hurts. It hurts that he still thinks of her, even in his dreams.

Jake's eyes suddenly fly open, and the smile on his face turns to terror. "Scarlett," he says in shock. "What are you doing?"

I slowly remove my lips from his cock and pull his waistband back over him.

I shake my head. "Nothing. It was nothing. Forget all about it. Go to bed. We can talk in the morning."

"Scarlett, wait. I didn't mean...I didn't know..."

I'm already halfway upstairs to my bedroom by the time Jake tells me to wait.

"It's really okay, Jake. I understand completely. I'm just tired now. I think it's best that we both just go to sleep."

"We can talk in the morning?"

I nod. "Sure."

I continue up the stairs, trying to forget about Jake. I open the door to my bedroom and close it behind me. I try to forget about what just happened because it was an honest mistake.

But, instead, all I keep thinking is, *This will never work.*

We don't belong together. He belongs with her, and I belong with Beast.

The only problem is, the people we're supposed to be with are too stubborn and stupid to realize that they belong with us.

25

BEAST

I KNOCK on Jake Walton's door. He agreed to meet me at his personal office at the financial firm he works for. Not in his office in Scarlett's building. I'm thankful because, if we had met in the same building as her office, it would have been too hard for me to resist the temptation. And, if I go see her again, I won't be able to resist.

"Come in," Jake says.

I open the door and let myself into a small office. I take everything in the second I walk through the door. I take in the white walls that he hasn't bothered to paint or decorate. I take in the standard desk that looks as boring as he does. I take in the picture frames sitting on the desk that look to be of his family, the only personal items he has in the office. I take in the neat pile of papers and almost spotless computer.

And then I take in the bastard sitting behind the desk. He's sharp-looking, despite his suit not being of the expensive type. His hair is nicely combed, and his face still looks clean-shaven, despite being late in the evening. He looks like a boy, not a man. He's young-looking, nice, and boring.

The very opposite of me.

"Nice to meet you, Mr. Hackett," Jake says as he stands from his desk and extends his hand to me.

I take his hand and shake it. I find his handshake to be far too weak for someone in the business world. I frown. "You, too, Jake."

Jake takes a seat. "So, you prefer to be called by your first name, Raymon?"

I take a seat opposite him. "No. I prefer to be called Mr. Hackett, Jake," I say, making sure to use *his* first name.

Jake narrows his eyes at me in return, but otherwise, he gives no impression that he finds my request unusual. "What can I do for you, Raymon?"

I smile, impressed at least that he has the balls to use my first name when I clearly told him to use my last. "I heard you're the best. I recently acquired a real estate company and would love your help in running the numbers on the company and making sure everything is in order."

Jake nods. "Have to be honest with you. Even though I am the best, my schedule is currently pretty busy. I recently took on several clients that will be taking up a lot of my time, and I'm not sure if I'll have time to put into the work you'd need me to do."

"Are you referring to your new job, working at Beautifully Bell Enterprises? Or are you referring to your recent relationship with the owner, Scarlett Bell?"

Jake glares at me, giving me such a heinous look that it should have me running scared out of his office. His look doesn't scare me though. His look just shows me how much of a weak man he really is. Because, if I were Jake and had any real claim to Scarlett and another guy came in and threatened that, there'd be no way that I'd just be sitting in a chair, giving him a dirty look. That man would already be ripped to shreds.

"It's none of your business. How do you know that anyway?" Jake says.

I lean back in my chair and smile. "I have my ways. And none of them are *your* business."

"I think we're through here," Jake says, getting up from his chair.

"Almost. I just have one final question."

Jake frowns, but hears me out anyway. That's a mistake.

"There are rumors that you don't do enough to satisfy Miss Bell. There are rumors that there is another man in her life other than you. Any idea if they are true or not?" I say with a smirk on my face.

I expect a sharp right hook to my jaw. I expect more cursed yelling for me to get the hell out of his office. I expect some sort of pain to be dealt by the hands of this man who is supposedly in love with Scarlett. Instead, I see a man raging with anger pick up his phone, and dial a number.

I raise my eyebrows, curious as to what he's doing. Because what he's doing is not on the list of things I would expect.

He begins talking, "I need security to come escort Mr. Hackett out of my office and make sure he's not allowed back on the property again."

My smile lightens. This man has more control over himself than I expected. The only problem is, he has no control over Scarlett. As much as he would like to lay claim to her, she's not his. She's *mine*. Or at least, she will be.

"No need. I'm leaving," I say with a grin on my face.

26

SCARLETT

I HEAR the knock on my apartment door, and I light up with a bright, albeit a nervous, smile on my face. Jake's sister is bringing her two young kids over for me and Jake to watch while she and her husband celebrate their anniversary in New York City.

When Jake said he would be watching his niece and nephew, I got excited because it meant I could see how he was around kids. It meant I could see how I would be around kids. Something that I haven't been around since… well, never. I don't have any siblings, and I didn't spend much time babysitting when I was younger.

I get up from the couch Jake and I have been sitting on while both working on our respective computers until the kids get here. Now, I'm on my feet as Jake walks to the door and opens it to his sister and niece and nephew.

"Good to see you, Nina. I missed you at the anniversary party," Jake says to his sister, wrapping his arms around her and the two kids in her arms. "Where's your husband?" he asks.

"Good to see you too. I was hoping we could have made

it to mom and dad's anniversary party, but then Claire was sick. And he's holding the cab for us," Nina answers.

She hands the rambunctious toddler with light-blond hair into Jake's hands. He takes him, happily throwing him up in the air, like he's nothing, and then catching him and spinning him around. The child squeals and laughs, as he seems happy to see his uncle.

Nina walks to the kitchen, still holding the brown-haired baby in her arm along with what I assume is a diaper bag slung over her shoulder. She sets the diaper bag on a counter in my kitchen and then walks over to me and hands me the baby. "This is Claire," Nina says.

I awkwardly hold the baby in my arms as she begins playing with my hair and pulling on my necklace. I try to keep the smile on my face. I try to keep the terror away, but I'm sure it's plastered all over my face. And I'm sure that Nina must be questioning her decision to leave her children with me even though Jake will be here as well.

She doesn't seem to care that she is leaving her kids in the hands of someone who knows nothing about kids. She walks back to the door and then pauses briefly. "We will be back around ten to collect the kids. If you need anything, you know my cell number. The kids will probably pass out around nine. Thanks again." And then she's out the door.

I look down at the baby in my arms and have no idea what to do. *Do I talk to her? Do I just hold her?* I should've brought some baby clothes from my line, and then at least we could've played dress-up.

"Balls," the toddler named Troy says.

I have no idea where he sees balls. I assume his mother packed some toys for him, so the balls he is referring to are probably in his bag that she dropped off.

I begin walking over to the bag, still holding the

baby in my arms, and I look for any toys for Troy. Troy, on the other hand, has a different idea as he begins climbing up onto my kitchen table. I now see what he meant when he said *balls*. He grabs the decorative balls out of the container on my kitchen table. Jake laughs and grabs the boy before he is able to climb all the way up.

The tot doesn't seem to care though, as he laughs more in his uncle's arms.

"You hungry?" Jake asks Troy.

Troy nods. "I want chicken nuggets."

"How about pizza?"

"Cheese?" Troy asks.

Jake nods.

"Okay," Troy says.

Jake goes over to the boxes of pizza that arrived just shortly before Troy and Claire. He begins fixing Troy something to eat while I just continue to awkwardly stand and stare at the baby.

After Jake gets Troy settled at the table with his pizza, he walks over to me. "Here, I'll hold her for a while, and you can eat your pizza." He has a smug grin on his face.

"What? What's so funny?" I ask.

He shakes his head, but continues to smile anyway. "Nothing. You're holding the baby like she is a priceless piece of art. Like, if you dropped her, she would break. You're not holding her like a baby."

I frown as I look at how I'm holding the baby tightly so that I don't drop her. I don't really see the problem with how I'm holding her. "If I drop her, she will break. What's wrong with the way I'm holding her?"

Jake takes Claire from my arms and holds her against his body. "Nothing. You're just funny."

I decide to let it go. I grab a slice of pepperoni pizza and take a seat next to Troy at my table.

I watch Jake wrinkle his nose, and then he checks her diaper. "I need to go change Claire's diaper and then make one quick phone call. You two going to be okay?"

"Yes," I say at the same time as Troy says, "Yes, Uncle Jake."

Jake smiles at both of us before he grabs the diaper bag and then heads to the spare bedroom to change her diaper and make the call. I turn my attention to my pizza and to Troy. I know I should say something to him. Ask him a question or entertain him somehow, but I have no idea what to talk about.

"I want ice cream," Troy says.

"You can have ice cream after you finish your pizza."

"I want ice cream now. No pizza."

I glance at his pizza. He's only taken two, maybe three, bites of his single slice.

"Once you finish your pizza, you can have ice cream," I say again, thinking the child will understand because I'm sure it's something his parents have said to him before. Boy, am I wrong.

Instead, Troy screams at the top of his lungs as tears fall from his eyes. "I don't want pizza! I want ice cream!"

I pat his back to try to get him to calm down, but it doesn't work. I glance toward the door to the bedroom Jake disappeared into to see if there are any signs that he is coming back anytime soon. There isn't. I'll have to handle this.

"Shh, it's gonna be okay. You can have ice cream soon."

"No, now!"

"How about you eat your pizza, like me?" I take another

bite of my pizza, trying to pretend like it's the most delicious food in the entire world.

Troy doesn't buy it though. This time, he screams and begins knocking his hands and feet against my table, making it shudder with each knock of his hands. The high-pitched squeal along with the thrashing is enough to drive a person mad. I have no idea how to calm him down other than to give in and give him the ice cream he wants.

"Okay, okay. I'll get you ice cream."

I get up from my chair and go to the freezer. I pull out the chocolate fudge pops we bought for him. I unwrap it quickly and hand it to Troy, who immediately stops crying as soon as he has the chocolate goodness in his hands. I sigh in relief and take a seat back at the kitchen table, hoping I can at least finish my one slice of pizza before I have to deal with the next crisis with him. That doesn't happen though. Instead, Troy decides he doesn't want us at the table anymore, and he jumps up before I can grab him.

"Troy, you have to sit at the table while you eat your ice cream."

"No!" Troy says as he runs to my living room and climbs up onto my white couch to eat his chocolate ice cream.

"Troy! Come back here right now," I say as I get up from the table, intending to get him to sit back down at the table.

But he squeals again when I try to grab him and bring him back to the table. And I know I'm not going to win. So, instead, I grab as many napkins as I can and my plate of pizza, and I join Troy on the couch where there's already two chocolate stains forming. I sigh. I wanted a new couch anyway. Because I don't have any faith that those chocolate stains are coming out of my white couch.

I hear the bedroom door open, and I turn to see Jake

walking back in with Claire in his arms along with a bottle. He laughs when he sees me and Troy.

"Troy, did you finish your pizza?" Jake asks.

"No." The boy looks down as redness fills his cheeks. "The lady said I could have ice cream."

Jake curiously raises his eyebrows at me, as if wondering what happened, but he just smiles and laughs and shakes his head at me.

"Troy, you need to finish your ice cream in the kitchen, and then you need to finish your slice of pizza."

"Okay," Troy says sadly as he makes his way back to the kitchen.

"How did you do that?" I ask.

Jake shakes his head as he sits down on the couch next to me. "He was just testing you to see what he could get away with."

I sigh. "And I failed big time."

Jake nods.

"It's my turn with Claire. You handle Troy," I say, knowing I have no chance at getting Troy to do anything I say.

Jake nods and hands me Claire along with her bottle. I hold her the same way Jake just was, cradling her in my arms, and then I take the bottle and hold it into her mouth. She begins to suck from it, and I sigh in relief because she is much easier to take care of than Troy was.

Jake stands up and heads to the kitchen, leaving me and Claire alone on the couch. She feeds from the bottle quietly, and I realize that she's really no trouble at all. I can handle this.

A few minutes later, Jake walks over, holding on to Troy's hand. "I'm going to give Troy a bath and try to wash the chocolate off of him."

I glance at Troy, who is truly covered in chocolate, all down the front of his shirt, his hands, and his face.

I nod, happy that I don't have to tackle bath time with a toddler.

"You and Claire going to be okay?"

"Yes," I say, looking down at the baby who is about to fall asleep as she feeds from her bottle. "I think we will be fine."

"Good. If you need anything, we'll be in the bathroom."

I watch as Jake leads Troy to the guest bathroom. I can't help but smile at the two of them. Jake is really good with him. Better than I expected.

I glance at Claire, who is just finishing her bottle. I remove the bottle from her lips, assuming she's done. Evidently, she wasn't done because she begins screaming shortly after.

"I'm sorry. I'm sorry," I say, hurriedly putting the bottle back into the baby's mouth. "Here you go."

But Claire doesn't want the bottle anymore. Apparently, she just wants to scream. I put the bottle down next to me and try to hold her closer to my body to get her to stop screaming. It doesn't work. I quickly stand up and begin trying to rock or bounce Claire in any way that might be calming. It doesn't work. I try singing. It doesn't work. I try bouncing in any sort of movement I can. But nothing works.

I try checking her diaper, just like Jake did, but that doesn't seem to be the problem. *I* seem to be the problem because I have no idea what to do.

So, I just continue walking around the room, trying to calm the baby that doesn't seem to be able to be calmed.

Until Jake walks back in the room with a cleaned up Troy and a goofy smile on his face. He walks over to me, and I immediately place Claire in his arms.

"I can't get her to stop crying," I say.

Jake nods and begins bouncing Claire up and down a little, but it doesn't work either. He then places her head against his shoulder, and he begins patting her on her back. She immediately burps and begins to calm down. My eyes widen.

"She just needed to be burped," Jake says.

Of course she did, I think to myself.

Of course, the woman who has never been around babies has no idea what to do with a baby after feeding it. I sigh and plop back down on the couch. Jake takes a seat next to me with this sleepy Claire in his arms, already looking like she's asleep the second he sits down.

"Troy, can you grab the remote that is sitting on the coffee table, and then I can put a movie on for you?" Jake says.

Troy grabs the remote and brings it to his uncle before climbing up on the couch next to him. Jake quickly puts on a movie for Troy, and Troy snuggles in next to Jake. Claire is sound asleep in his arms. And I'm left sitting by myself, feeling like there's no way I could ever have kids by myself. The only way I could ever have kids is with a man like Jake. Because I have no idea how to handle kids.

I snuggle up to Jake's other side and close my eyes, ready for the day to be over. Ready to get back to my office tomorrow where I feel like I have some semblance of control. Ready to get back to my office tomorrow where I know what the hell I'm doing. Because, right now, I feel clueless.

27

BEAST

IT'S a stupid mistake that I've only made once before. But I have to be sure. I have to be sure that she is worth risking my life for. I have to see her in the daylight, face-to-face. I have to see her and see that she really wants me and not him. Because I'm already sure that he's not good enough for her. I'm just not sure if she believes that she's better than him.

I walk into Beautifully Bell Enterprises along with my team of two men. None of my men know why we're really here. They just think we are here on another job. Scouting out another woman. Another company. They don't know that this job didn't come from the boss. They came for me, and it has nothing to do with what our boss wants. It only has to do with what I want.

Thankfully, my men trust me and will do whatever I ask, whenever I ask. No questions asked. I guess that's the one perk of my job.

We walk up to the floor where Scarlett's office sits.

Scarlett's assistant called back to tell us her decision if she was going to take our financial advice or not and use us in the future. But I managed to arrange the meeting so that she could give us the decision in person. I already know her answer though. I already know she chose Jake as her financial manager, and that's fine. I'm not here to try to convince her to use my company instead.

I already know that she's a smart businesswoman who doesn't need our financial advice. Her assistant tried to tell us her decision over the phone, and I said that we needed to be told in person that she wouldn't be needing our services. It was just an excuse to see her again.

Nerves creep up inside me as we walk closer and closer to where I know her office is. I know this is a risk. I know that, when she sees me this time, she might recognize me. She might realize who I am. Even the last time was a risk, but she hardly looked at me then. It was obvious she was still blissfully thinking about our night together and not thinking that I could be in the same room as her.

This time though, she knows me better. She might recognize my voice. She's seen my eyes. She knows my body. And I know, inside her head, she's formed some sort of image of what I look like, and if that image at all matches what I truly look like, then I'm fucked. Because this is not how I want her to figure out who I am. This is just me figuring out what I want.

So, I let my men take the lead as we approach her office. Dustin, my more trusted man, knocks on her office door, and her assistant comes out and leads us into her office where they've been waiting.

Scarlett begins shaking everyone's hands. It's when I realize that I'm going to get to touch her skin again. I silently wait my turn until she gets to me. When she does, I keep my eyes from hers as I feel her smooth skin against my rough hand. She doesn't treat me any differently than any of the previous men, and it's when I know that she doesn't recognize me.

I watch Scarlett walk back behind her desk, and Preston takes a seat next to her.

"When you contacted us for a follow-up, Preston really should've told you that it wasn't necessary for all three of you to come back down here again. I just wanted to inform you of our decision and say thank you for being so kind. I think you are a fantastic firm, but we decided to go in a different direction."

I want to speak, but I don't. I know that the more I limit my voice, the less likely it is that she will be able to recognize me. So, I don't speak.

Instead, I let Dustin speak, "It's really not a problem. We wanted to come down here and make sure that you didn't want to take us up on our offer. Because we believe that we could really help you take your business to the next level."

Scarlett smiles at Dustin, and I lose it. I want her smiling at me, not him. I scoot my chair on the hard floor, causing it to make a loud scraping sound. But it gives me the attention I want. It gives me Scarlett's eyes back on me and not him. She warmly smiles at me for just a second and then turns her attention back to Dustin.

"I really appreciate it, Mr. Morgan. I really appreciate all that your men have done. And, if I ever decide that I need help with growing the business, I will gladly take you up on your offer. At the moment, I feel that we have one of the best financial managers in the world, and I feel like he's going to do a fantastic job. If I change my mind though, you will be my first call because you have my confidence that you are the best man for the job. You were just beat out slightly by another."

She stands, and I know the meeting is over. I know that

this is my last chance to assess her. To determine if she's worth it. But I already know my answer. I already know that my heart is racing. I already know that, just by coming here, I've risked everything, and I've already made up my mind. She's worth the risk.

Scarlett begins shaking each of our hands again. I wait my turn for one last touch of her skin before I do the stupidest thing I've ever done. Risk my life.

She gets to me, and this time, I don't look down.

I look right into her eyes. "It was a pleasure, Miss Bell."

I shake her hand, and she looks at me with a hint of confusion on her face.

"It was nice speaking with you as well, Mr. Guild."

I turn and follow my men out of her office, hating the name that fell from her lips when she was referring to me. I hate that the only name I've ever heard fall from her lips, other than Beast, is a fake name. It's not my real name. But I don't know if my real name falling from her lips would be any better. I just want to hear the one name she's adapted for me from her lips again as I claim her and make her mine. I just want her to call me Beast again.

28

SCARLETT

I RUN. *I run faster and faster, trying to escape the darkness. But the darkness continues to find me, continues to chase me, until there is nothing left of me.*

But I keep running anyway. I keep running, trying to escape the darkness I've found myself in. I try to escape even though I know there's no use. I've let the darkness into my heart, and now, there's no way to get it out.

Kinsley has been taken from me. I let the darkness consume her. I let the darkness take her from me, and now, I'm alone. And she's in danger. And there's nothing I can do to save her. Still, I run to try to save her.

The darkness pushes Jake away. Keeping Jake away from me but keeping him safe. He tries to pull me back to keep me from running, but still, I keep running.

The darkness consumes Preston's soul. It intertwines in his head, scaring him with the thoughts that the darkness is taking me away from him. That I'm in danger even if I'm not. Preston pushes me to run while still being scared and thinking I shouldn't.

Worst of all, Beast is affected by the darkness. It's so

connected to him that it's hard to tell what's the darkness and what's him. I run because Beast tells me to run. But he doesn't tell me why I am running.

Me. The darkness pulls at me, and I go willingly. I run.

All of us are connected through the darkness. Through a past and a future that I don't understand. Still, I try to connect the pieces. Kinsley. Jake. Beast. Preston. And me. They're all connected. I just don't understand how.

I OPEN my eyes and stretch, trying to put the strange dream I just had behind me. It was just a dream. And nothing really happened in the dream. I was running. I remember that. I remember everyone who's important in my life appearing in my dream. I just don't understand what any of it means.

I try to push the dream out of my head because today's going to be a good day. Today, I'm taking Kinsley out to plan her baby shower. I know it's still early, but I want to throw her the best baby shower that's ever been thrown. And I know that it's going to take a lot of planning. Plus, I'll take any excuse not to think about the men in my life and just focus on my good friend for at least an afternoon.

I head to my shower and take my time in getting ready. Showering, dressing, and doing my hair and makeup. There's no reason to hurry today. I don't plan on going into work. I'll just answer some emails from my computer. And all that's waiting for me downstairs is Jake.

He's been staying with me since his fiancée kicked him out of their apartment. He just hasn't been sleeping in my bed with me. Yet. He said he was going to look for another apartment, but I know we've both been stalling, not wanting him to get a new apartment until we decide if this thing between us is really going to work out or not. If it does, he can just stay here with me.

When I finally finish getting ready, I head downstairs. I look around my living room for any signs of Jake, but there's none to be found. I frown. I'm so used to seeing Jake greet me at the base of the stairs every morning with coffee and breakfast, just like he used to do when we were in college. In fact, I have gotten a little spoiled from having him live here. It looks like, this Saturday morning, he's either sleeping in or decided I'm not worth the effort.

I head to the kitchen to make myself breakfast when I see a note on the counter along with a paper bag. I pick up the note and read it.

Scarlett,

I had to go meet with some clients today for work. I wasn't sure what time you'd get up, but the coffee should still be hot in the pot. There are also some bagels in the bag. Have a good day with Kinsley.

With love,

Jake

I smile as I read the note, happy that he didn't forget about my breakfast. Happy that he remembered to take care of me. I glance at the bottom where the words, *With love,* stand out. It's not weird that he wrote it. Lots of people I know write that at the end of notes. It doesn't mean he's *in* love with me. It doesn't mean he *isn't* in love either.

I sigh and place the note back on the counter, trying not to read too much into it. I'm not ready for him to love me yet. All I want is a few dates to see if there is more to him than just being able to care for me. Because, although it's nice, I don't need anyone taking care of me. I've been taking care of myself since I was thirteen. What I want is a partner, lover, challenger.

I fix my breakfast and get my computer. I decide to eat outside on my balcony this morning while I work. My phone buzzes in my pocket, and I pull it out to look at it. When I see whom the message is from, I drop my phone. I watch it clank against the hard floor.

Shit.

I stare at the phone on the floor, thankful that it didn't shatter, although I'm sure it has a few good scratches on it now. I want to pick it up, but I don't.

It's from Beast. I'm afraid of what the text says. I'm afraid he's just going to go back to texting me, like nothing happened. And I can't give him that without more. I'm also afraid that he's going to say he's willing to give me more even though I've already closed off my heart to him. Even though I've already decided on Jake.

So, I just stare. As my heartbeat races. Faster. Faster. Faster. Until I can hear my heart pumping in my chest. Until my breathing becomes loud and uneven. And until I'm afraid I'm going to give myself a heart attack if I don't pick up my damn phone.

I slowly bend down and cautiously grab the phone, like it's a scared dog that might bite if I'm not too careful with it. I study the phone for a second, and as I look, there seems to be a few scratches on the screen and back. But, somehow, the screen managed to stay unshattered.

I unlock my phone and hover over the message from Beast. I could just delete it. I could forget this ever happened.

I shake my head. *No way in hell.*

I open the message and read.

Beast: I was wrong.

That's all the bastard says. *I was wrong.*

I read his words over and over, trying to find the

meaning behind them. There are too many things that he could mean with that statement, and I don't even know where to begin. He could be wrong about letting me go. He could be wrong about telling me who he is. Or he could be wrong about wanting me in the first place.

I consider texting him back to ask him what he means. But I'm afraid I won't get a straight answer. He's obviously not ready to tell me what he's wrong about. He just texted me to drive me crazy until he's ready to tell me.

I want to throw my phone over the balcony and watch it shatter on the sidewalk below. I don't, as much as I want to. I want to forget he ever existed. I want to erase that night from my memory. I want to go back in time and say no instead of yes. Maybe then I wouldn't have to feel this pain every time he texts me. Every time he does, it affects my life. Because that's what he's doing when he's texting me. He's pulling me back away from the decision I've made to be with Jake yet not giving me everything I want with him. He's an asshole.

My phone buzzes again in my hand, and I jump because, despite how much I hate him, I hope it's him. I hope it's him texting me more than *I was wrong*. When the phone buzzes again though, I realize it's not a text message; it's a phone call. From Kinsley.

I hit Answer. "Hey, babe!" I say as happily as I can, trying to forget all about Beast.

"Hey! You ready? I know I'm a bit early, but I'm excited," Kinsley says.

"Yes! I'm absolutely ready," I say. I begin cleaning up my breakfast and my computer as I continue holding my phone against my ear.

"Good. I'm waiting for you downstairs."

I laugh. "I'll be right down."

I quickly clean up, get my purse, reluctantly stick my phone into my purse, and head downstairs to meet my best friend. When I get off the elevator, Kinsley is standing at the bottom with a huge grin on her face. I merely wrap my arms around her.

"You have no idea how excited I am!"

I smile. "What? You're excited? I couldn't tell," I joke with her.

She playfully hits me on the shoulder. "I know. I'm sorry. Killian's just driving me nuts."

I frown. "What? Now, what did Killian do?"

Kinsley rolls her eyes at me. "No, nothing like that. He's just being overprotective of me and this baby. Will hardly let me do anything around the house anymore. Won't let me go to work. If it were up to him, he'd put me on bed rest and never let me leave the house again."

I laugh. "He's just trying to protect you and make sure you and the baby are safe."

"I know. It's why I love him. I just need a break from him."

"Good. Because I need a break from all men."

Kinsley laughs. "Good. I can't wait to hear all the juicy details."

"Before we start in on all the juicy details, we should get going. We have the cake shop to visit. The caterer. We need to talk decorations. And, of course, to visit several baby shops. All in one day."

Kinsley nods, but I can tell the excitement isn't going away anytime soon. That she really needs today. That she really needs a break from her husband and to just be able to relax for once. And that's exactly what I plan on giving her.

"You okay having my driver, George, drive us?" I ask.

"Yes!" Kinsley squeals, unable to say anything without showing her excitement.

I smile and grab her hand. "Let's go."

We walk out of my building and over to where George sits, waiting for us.

"Good morning, girls," George says as he opens the door for us to climb into the car.

"Good morning," we both say back.

We both climb in as well as George.

"Where to?" he asks.

I glance at Kinsley and then down at the clock in the car, reading the time. It's only nine o'clock, but I know exactly where Kinsley's going to want to go first. Her favorite part of this baby-shower planning.

"Cake shop first," I say.

George smiles at me, and then he pulls the car away from the curb and begins driving us. Kinsley smiles brightly beside me, unable to contain her excitement.

"So, tell me about these damn men you are trying to forget about today."

I sigh. "I'd rather not. I just want to forget they exist and have a good day with my bestie."

"I want to—" Kinsley grabs ahold of her stomach as a pained look comes over her face.

I turn and grab her shoulders, trying to comfort her. "Are you okay?"

I meet George's eyes in the mirror and see that he's prepared to take us to the nearest hospital. Kinsley takes a deep breath and then another and another. Ignoring me, just focusing on her breathing. Time is moving slowly, and I'm worried that something is seriously wrong.

My eyes move back up to George, and I'm about ready to tell him to head to the nearest hospital when Kinsley says,

"I'm fine. I just didn't eat breakfast this morning, and I'm pretty sure this little one is telling me he or she is hungry. I'll be fine after I get some cake in me."

I study my friend for a couple of moments more until she's breathing normally again, and that goofy smile has returned to her face.

"George, can you—"

"Already on it, Miss Scarlett," George says.

I glance up with a smile as I see that George is already pulling us into the drive-through of the nearest Starbucks. That's why I love George so much. He can read my mind, and he knows exactly what I want before I even have to ask it. He knew I'd want to make sure Kinsley got breakfast before I took her to the cake shop.

After a quick Starbucks run to get Kinsley a breakfast sandwich, we're back on the road, driving toward the cake shop.

Between bites of her breakfast sandwich, Kinsley says, "You still never told me about the men you're trying to forget about. What's going on?"

"It's nothing. Nothing I want to talk about anyway."

Kinsley takes another bite. And, with a mouthful, she says, "Tell me what's going on. It will make me feel better."

I narrow my eyes at her, afraid she's going to take this pregnancy thing and use it to her advantage. I need to be better prepared in the future to deal with her scheming. But, for right now, I'll give in to her. Right now, I'll give her exactly what she wants, as she knows I don't want to see her in pain or upset.

"I just want both men to be something they're not. I want Jake to challenge me more, to live a little more danger-ously. And I want..." I stop, not sure what to call Beast in front of Kinsley.

"You want your one-night-stand guy?"

"I want him to want more than one night. I want him to want a real relationship and to care for me just a little bit. Is that too much to ask of the two men in my life? For one of them to step up and be the complete package?"

Kinsley puts the rest of her sandwich on her lap and shakes her head. "No, it's not too much to ask of them. And if neither one of them can give you that, perhaps it's time to let both of them go."

I nod, knowing she's right. "I'm just tired of being alone. I'm ready to move on with my life."

Kinsley wraps her arms around me, and she holds my head tight to her chest. "You're not alone, Scar. You have me and always will. And you'll have a niece or a nephew to keep you busy soon."

I smile and pat her belly. "You're right. After this baby is born, I'll be spending all my time with him or her. I won't even be thinking about men."

The rest of the day, we don't talk about men. We don't talk about Killian, Jake, or Beast. We don't even talk about Preston. We just focus on each other, and the baby's party we are planning.

We test about one million cakes at the cake shop. Finally, we settle on three flavors—wedding cake, strawberry shortcake, and chocolate-cookie filling.

At the caterer, we decide on a full buffet filled with everything from tacos to Italian to burgers. Kinsley said we should just pick one. But there was no way I'd let her pick just one, not when we are celebrating her baby. She deserves the best, and that's exactly what I plan on giving her.

We discuss some decoration options and things that Kinsley likes and doesn't like. But I don't want her to be heavily involved in the decorations or activities for the baby shower. I want to plan some things that will be a surprise to her. She'll just have to wait to find out what I have planned.

The last stop for the day is a cute boutique where she can begin registering for gifts for the baby. This shower isn't going to happen for at least three months, but still, she needs to start registering for gifts. Mostly because it's one of the most fun parts about a baby shower.

"This is going to have to be the last stop. I'm exhausted. My feet are swollen. My back is killing me," Kinsley says.

I smile at her. "You know it's only going to get worse from here, right? You're not even halfway through yet. Just imagine how exhausted you will feel a few months from now."

"Don't remind me."

"We don't have to go. I can just have George drive us back to your apartment. We can schedule another day to come to this boutique."

"No, no. I want to look at the cute onesies and baby shoes and things."

I wrinkle my nose. "Babies need shoes? Doesn't it take them a few years to learn to walk?"

Kinsley laughs. "Not a few years. A few months to one year. And the shoes aren't for walking. They're just cute. I thought you of all people would understand accessorizing and just looking cute."

"I understand looking cute for cute's sake. Just curious."

I follow Kinsley into the boutique, and I'm amazed by the smells and sights I see the second we're in the store. It smells like baby in here.

And, immediately, when I look around the store, it gives me all sorts of ideas and plans to start my own baby line. Kinsley immediately walks over toward the clothes section, and I follow. We go through every dress in the store, oohing and aahing over our favorites. I already know I will be getting her baby basically this whole store, plus whatever I end up having designed for the baby.

"This baby is going to be the most spoiled baby on the planet," I say.

"I know. Between you dressing my baby and Killian giving it everything that it could ever want, I'm afraid our baby is gonna turn into one spoiled brat."

"The baby will just be the most well-dressed baby who has everything they could ever imagine. It will be the most loved baby in the entire world."

"Maybe you're right."

"Of course I'm right. I'm always right."

"I'm going to go to the restroom. Be right back," Kinsley says.

"I'll be right here, salivating over all the adorable little things, as my ovaries burst with need, wanting a baby."

"You do that. My evil plan is working," she says.

"What do you mean?" I call after her.

"I just knew, the second I got you around all this baby stuff, that you would want to have a baby yourself. And having a baby would be a million times more fun if you were having one as well," she says before walking away from me.

I roll my eyes because I don't want to let her know that she's winning. That she's already won, and she's already convinced me that I want a baby, too. Because it's something I've been thinking about forever. Even through all the one-night stands. I just can't have one alone, and I'm not sure either of the two men in my life is the right choice.

I get lost in my head, thinking about all the designs that I want to discuss with my design team when I get back to the office, while Kinsley's in the restroom. I walk over to one of the cashiers and ask if they have some paper and a pencil. She gladly hands them over to me, and I began sketching some ideas that have been floating around in my head of things that could work for a baby line.

I get so lost in sketching and designing that I don't know how long Kinsley's been gone. When I notice I've done about a half-dozen designs, I stick the papers into my purse and begin scanning the store, looking for Kinsley. I don't see her anywhere.

I walk over to the cashier. "Have you seen my friend?"

The cashier shakes her head. I begin walking again, but don't see her. The boutique is pretty small, so it's not like she could be hiding anywhere. I walk to the restroom and push the door open. My mouth drops open as I see Kinsley lying on the floor, holding her stomach.

"Oh my God! What's wrong?"

"My stomach," is all she can get out as she moans and twists her body on the ground.

I rush to her side and grab her hand that she begins to squeeze tightly. My purse drops to the floor, and I dig out my cell phone with a shaking hand.

"I'm scared," she whispers.

And I panic. I don't know what the fuck is happening, but I know it's bad.

"Just squeeze my hand, and everything's gonna be okay. I'm going to make everything okay."

Kinsley moans louder as I grab for my phone again. I unlock it and see that Beast texted me again. I ignore it, not giving a fuck about what he has to say. I dial 911 and hold the phone to my ear.

"Nine-one-one. What's your emergency?"

"My friend. She's on the restroom floor in a boutique,

and she's in a lot of pain. She's pregnant." I try to keep my voice calm and steady, so as not to let Kinsley know that anything is wrong. Although I know she can hear it. She knows me better than anyone else.

"Okay. Is she breathing? Is she awake?"

"Yes."

"Good. I need you to tell me the address, and then I'll have an ambulance on its way. I need you to just keep her awake and calm. I need you to tell me if she stops breathing or passes out, okay?"

I nod, not able to answer her question.

"Okay?" the operator says more firmly.

"Okay." I tell the operator the address.

Then, I wait as I hold Kinsley's hand until the ambulance arrives with the paramedics. I feel completely useless as I sit next to her, holding her hand, praying like hell that nothing happens to her or this baby. Because I don't know what I would do if something did.

29

BEAST

I SEE MY MARK. I've studied her. I understand her—or at least as well as I'll ever understand another woman. I know what I have to do. I know what I have to do to get her alone. I know what I have to do to take her out.

All I have to do now is report the plan to my boss. Tell her how and when I plan on taking her out. Then, I'll get the go-ahead, and it'll happen. Just like it has happened hundreds of times before.

I don't know why this one is hard for me. I've killed before. Too many times to count. I don't even care about this woman. She's nothing to me. But I feel reluctant to take on this job. To kill this woman.

I shouldn't feel reluctant though. If anything, I should want revenge. And the revenge would be justified because of what she's done to me in my life. I should want to end her life. I should want to end her life in the same way that she ended mine.

Still, as I watch her, my heart fills with pain at the thought of pulling the trigger. I don't know if my reluctance to kill her is because I no longer want to be a killer. Or if it's because of Scarlett. Because I don't want to hurt her. I don't want to be a killer even though that's what I am.

I am a killer.

That's what I do for work. But it's more than just that. It's *who* I am. It's *why* I wake up in the morning. It's *why* I sleep well at night. I kill those who need to be killed. I kill those who have done me or my family wrong.

I kill. And I enjoy it.

Until now...

30

SCARLETT

I HATE WAITING. I have no patience for waiting. I hate giving up that control. But I don't really have a choice. My only choice is to wait.

I rode with Kinsley in the ambulance to the hospital. I held her hand the entire time. Terrified that something was going to happen. I watched as the paramedics worked on her, but didn't tell me what was going on. They just worked tirelessly, trying to solve a problem that I didn't understand.

I stayed with her right up until we got to the hospital. They took her to another room and told me to wait.

So, here I am, in the waiting room, waiting.

At first, I had something to do. I called Killian and told him to get here right away. When he got here, he spoke to me briefly. He spent the rest of the time arguing with doctors until they finally let him go back to see her. I haven't seen him since, and they haven't let me go back yet or given me any updates on how she's doing.

I spend the rest of my time staring into space. I consider texting Jake to let him know that I need him. That I need him to come be with me, to comfort me. But I'm just not sure if him being here would actually bring me any comfort. So, I don't text him—at least, not yet.

I still have an unread message from Beast taunting me. Every time I open my phone, I see the red little number one on the Messages app, telling me I have a missed message. Telling me that Beast has something to say to me. Telling me that, if I would just open it, he could finally give me the answer I'd been wanting all along. Or he could twist the dagger that's already in my heart.

It's been hours now since we showed up at the hospital. Far too long for me to just sit and do nothing. I have to do something.

I open my phone. I open a new message and text Jake.

Me: Kinsley's at the hospital. I'm not sure what's wrong yet. Just waiting.

I give Jake a chance to prove to me that he's the guy for me. But I also want to give Beast the same chance. So, I open the unread message.

Beast: I want to tell you who I am.

I don't know if it's the emotion from the day finally getting to me or if I really care that much about knowing who Beast is. But I cry when I see the message. I ugly cry. The kind of crying that you usually do when you're alone in your bedroom. Not the kind of crying you do in a public hospital, especially not one that deals with loss on a daily basis.

A nurse immediately comes over to me, thinking I got some horrible news about a family member. She sits next to me and places her hand on my back. "If you need someone to talk to, there are pastors and ministers that I could arrange to talk with you. Or I could just talk to you?"

I shake my head. "I'm sorry." I wipe my eyes, trying to stop the crying. "Really, I'm fine. I just got some happy news, and that mixed with my anxiety and feelings of not knowing what's going on with my best friend. It caused the tears."

The nurse nods in understanding, but doesn't stop rubbing my back until the tears have fully diminished. "That's pretty normal. People cry here for all sorts of reasons. My advice is to just cry and get out. Don't hold the emotion in."

"Thanks," I say.

I take a few deep breaths, and then the nurse leaves me alone. I go back to my text message.

Me: Kinsley, my best friend, is in the hospital. I don't know what's wrong with her, but I'm afraid it's serious. I'm here, waiting.

I close my phone after sending the text message to Beast. And then I wait. I wait to find out what's wrong with Kinsley. And I wait to find out if either of the men will prove to me that I should be with one of them. Or if I should be alone.

I don't have to wait much longer to get at least one of my answers.

"Scarlett," Killian says.

I look up and see Killian standing over me with tears in his eyes. His face is red and puffy. He looks like he's just gone through hell and back. I jump up, needing to know that she's still alive. Needing to know that she's okay.

"Is she..." I ask, unable to finish that sentence.

I was told my best friend died once before. That pain was unbearable. If I'm told that again, I don't think I could survive, no matter if either of those men showed up to help me.

"She's..." Killian takes a deep breath, like he can't quite

get it out, and then I wrap my arms around him as we both cry again. "Alive," he whispers into my ear.

But it doesn't stop our sobs or my feeling that something is wrong. I know, if he's been crying, there is something wrong. We just cry and hold each other for a long time. For too long. Neither one of us wants to let go. Neither one of us wants to go face what I'm afraid just happened.

"She needs you to go see her, Scarlett. She needs her best friend. I did the best I could to help her. And I'm not sure how much help I'm being when I'm in just as much pain myself," Killian says.

We slowly pull away from each other.

"I don't know if I can help her." My voice is shaky. *I'm not strong enough for this.*

"Yes, you can. You're one of the strongest people I know. Now, go help your best friend," Killian says sternly, giving me the intense glare that he always does whenever he's around someone who isn't Kinsley.

He's right. I am strong. And I have to be strong for her.

I leave Killian standing in the waiting room, and I walk to the room number he gave me. I knock softly on the door and immediately open it, not waiting until I lose my nerve to go in. I see Kinsley lying in a hospital bed, connected to all sorts of machines and tubes. I quickly walk over to her and throw my arms around her, holding her in a strong, tight embrace.

I feel her tears dripping onto my back, and I feel my own tears dripping down my face and onto hers. We hold each other for a long time. Longer than I held on to Killian. I don't ask her what happened. I already know. I know from the look on Killian's face. I know from the look on hers when I entered the room. I know from the way she's hugging me.

I won't ask, not unless she needs to tell me. Not unless she needs to say the words out loud in order to heal.

I don't bother with words at all really. I know that no words I could say at this moment would erase the pain that she's feeling. Because I can feel the pain that she's feeling with every ounce of my being as I hold on to her. It's horrible pain. It's the worst kind of pain. It's the most intense pain ever felt, even worse than when I thought I had lost her.

We hold on to each other for who knows how much longer. Killian eventually comes into the room and sits behind his wife, holding on to her as well. We both just hold her until she's finally ready to speak.

"It was a boy."

Our sobs deepen at her words. I try to think of something to say, but I can't.

"His name was Wesley."

We sob some more.

We let the pain consume us.

We let the love for a child that we will never get to meet surround us.

I want to run. I want to run away from all the pain and heartache. Unlike my dream, I don't run though. I stay right here where I belong. I stay in the darkness.

31

SCARLETT

I OPEN my eyes and lift my neck off the arm of the chair that I must've slept on. As I sit up, I feel a shooting pain in my neck. I slowly stretch it, trying to make the pain in my neck go away. It doesn't go away easily, but as I continue to stretch, it does become more tolerable. Tolerable enough that I can sit up in the chair.

I glance around the room, trying to figure out where I am. It's still relatively dark in the room, despite the morning light seeping in through the blinds. I see Kinsley asleep in a hospital bed, and then I remember. I remember the horrible reason we're here. I glance over at Killian, who is sitting in a chair next to his wife's hospital bed, just staring at her.

"Good morning. Do you need anything? Does she need anything?" I say.

"No. At least, we don't need anything that you can get us right now," Killian says, his voice seeming more distant than it did yesterday.

I run my hand through my hair as I stare at Kinsley sleeping in the hospital room.

We both stayed with her all day yesterday and all through the night. And I'm afraid that we didn't do anything to make it better for her or for us. I rub my eyes, and I can still feel the sting from my tears. I can feel the swollenness in my eyes from crying all day and through the night. The pain is here just as badly as it was yesterday. And it's not going away anytime soon.

I know that going to get coffee or breakfast for us isn't really going to help. That the pain will still be here. But it's something that I can do.

So, I get up from the chair. "I'm going to get us coffee and breakfast. I'll be back soon."

I don't wait for Killian to answer me. I know that, even if he does, it'll be a distant speech about how breakfast won't fix anything. And I understand that, but it will give me some purpose. It will give me something to do.

I walk out of her hospital room and close the door, finally feeling like I can breathe a little the second I step out. I lean against the door, put my head in my arms, and just try to breathe. The tears come from me again, and I cry and cry and cry. I hate that I can't fix this for her. I hate that I can't bring back her baby.

It takes a while, but when the tears finally subside a little, I stand off the door and walk toward the elevator. I take the elevator down to the main floor where there is supposedly a cafeteria, according to the signs. I walk to the cafeteria and see that they have all sorts of breakfast items and coffees. I know it's not going to be the best breakfast we've ever had. But I know that even the best breakfast wouldn't do much to heal our souls.

So, instead, I get in line, and I get a few options—bagels, eggs, toast, and fruit. I don't really know if any of us are going to feel like eating, but simple, boring food might help.

I put all the items on a tray, followed by three coffees, and then I slowly work my way back upstairs to Kinsley's room.

I have to really focus with each step that I take to ensure that I don't drop any of the food or spill any of the coffee. It's really nice to be able to focus on something so intently that isn't pain. With each step that I take, I become more and more focused. With each step that I take, the tiniest part of the pain becomes erased from my mind, replaced with more and more need to focus. I spill a little bit of the coffee as I take a step, but it just refocuses me more until I forget why we're even at this hospital.

Until I reach Kinsley's hospital door.

Sitting on the floor outside of it is Jake. I give a weak smile at him, thankful that he finally came. He doesn't smile back. He just stands from his place on the floor and opens the door for me.

As I walk past, he says, "We need to talk."

I nod my head at him. "I'll be right back," I say.

I walk into Kinsley's bedroom, surprised to see that she's still asleep. She is always an early riser. But the loss she dealt with yesterday has taken a lot from her. And the nurses gave her some meds to help her sleep last night. Killian is still sitting next to her, right where I left him.

"I brought breakfast. You don't have to eat it. But it's here if you decide to," I say as I set the tray down on one of the tables in her room.

Killian nods but doesn't say anything. I grab one of the coffees and take it with me back outside to speak with Jake.

When I walk back into the hallway, Jake is still waiting for me with the same frown on his face.

"How is she doing?" he asks.

I study my coffee, hating the question. Afraid that, if I let myself think too much about Kinsley, I'll cry again. "Not well."

"I'm sorry."

I nod, trying to keep my words to a minimum.

"How are you doing?"

"Not much better." I look up at him, and I see the sadness in his eyes, but I also see something else that I'm not used to seeing from him. Anger.

"Why didn't you come yesterday?" I ask.

He pauses. "I did. At first, they wouldn't let me come to her room. And I didn't want to text you and disturb you. Eventually, they let me up, but by then, you'd all passed out. I stayed for a while and then went home, determined to come back first thing this morning."

I try to smile at him again, but I just can't. And I'm tired of waiting for him to spell out whatever he came here to say. I've been through too much in the last twenty-four hours to be able to handle anything more.

"Just tell me. Tell me whatever you came here to say," I say, feeling exhausted.

Jake takes a deep breath and then another before he reaches into his pocket and pulls out my phone. My eyes zoom in on the phone in his hands. It's my phone. I must've left it when I went downstairs to get breakfast.

I reach for the phone. "Thanks."

I don't understand why he seems angry to be giving me my phone back.

He doesn't let me take my phone back though. Instead, he unlocks the phone and pulls up something on it before he hands it to me. The screen is opened to message after message from Beast. Each message contains our dirty desires. Each message is filled with my need for more from him. Each message is filled with the truth of need and want.

"Who is Beast?" Jake asks.

I frown as I look at the phone. I can't believe he's going to cause a fight about this now.

"Really? You're going to bring this up now? You're going to do anything but try to be here for me when my heart is completely broken and shattered from dealing with the loss I dealt with yesterday? When I'm this fucking broken? That's when you choose to start a fight over a text message that you shouldn't have seen anyway because you shouldn't have been snooping on my phone."

Jake takes a step toward me. "No, I'm not starting a fight. All I want to know is, who is Beast?"

I take a step toward Jake, letting my anger mix with the pain in such a way that I'm afraid of saying things that I don't mean. No, that's not true. Maybe I'll say exactly what I mean, and the anger and pain won't stop me. I have no filter.

"He's a man I fucked before you. He's a man who brought out desires I never knew I had. He's a man I've wanted because *you* haven't given me anything other than nice."

"What's his name?" Jake asks.

"I don't know."

He shakes his head. "Tell me his name," he says more sternly.

"I don't know," I repeat again more slowly and just as sternly as his voice was.

I see the anger explode in Jake's eyes.

"Don't fucking lie to me! Just tell me who he is."

"I. Don't. Know."

Jake runs his hands through his hair as he starts pacing back and forth in the hallway. "Do you love me?"

I think for a moment. *Do I love him?* "Yes," I answer honestly.

I do love Jake. At least on some level. My heart wouldn't be in so much pain right now, thinking about not having a real chance with him if this conversation continues the way that I know it's going to.

Jake pauses, listening to my words. "Do you love him?"

"Yes."

"How is that fucking possible? How can you love two men at the same time?"

I shake my head. "I don't know. I just do. Maybe because neither one of you has given me everything I need. All you've given me are parts of yourself, and although I've fallen just a little bit for each of your parts, it's not real. Because neither of you has given me what I need."

"And what's that? How am I supposed to know what you want when you won't tell me?"

"I have told you. You just don't listen."

"I don't know what it has to do with you and me," Jake says, pointing to my phone. "I don't know how we are supposed to keep dating if you lie to me."

"I didn't lie. I never fucked him when I was dating you. It was all before."

"Yeah, you just texted him all the dirty things you wished he would do while you were with *me*."

I feel the tears starting again, but I keep them back. I'm not going to let him make me feel bad. Not right now. Not when there are more important things that need to be handled. This should be a time of us getting closer, not a time of us pulling apart.

A thought Preston said to me earlier creeps back into my mind and I have to know. "Is Karissa real?"

"What?"

I raise my eyebrows. "Is she real?"

"Of course she is real!"

I shake my head. "I don't believe you."

He narrows his eyes at me and I can see him trying to determine how best to hurt me like I've hurt him. I know I've hurt him in the past when I broke up with him the first time. I saw the pain, but I realize now that was for the best. That day was so painful when I realized he wasn't the man for me. I didn't break up with him because I was afraid of commitment. I broke up with him because he was weak. He wasn't strong enough to handle me.

I kiss his ear. "Do me in the bathroom," I whisper into Jake's ear.

He shrugs me off. "No, Scarlett."

I pout my bottom lip. "Oh come on. Live a little."

He gives me a stern look. "No." He lifts the beer to his lips while we stand next to the same pub table we stood at on our first date. Months have passed, but nothing's changed.

I lift my own beer to my lips. I'm not going to let him off that easy. I run my hand through my hair and push my breasts out making sure he can see what he is missing as he stands all stoic and gentleman like across the table from me. Except I don't want a gentleman, at least not in every aspect. I want a man. One that's rough, dangerous, and takes care of me even when I don't need it.

I feel someone pinch my ass, I look over at Jake but his hands are both firmly on the table. I turn to see who the man is that just pinched my ass as he walks past us acting like he didn't just do something wrong.

"Hey jackass!" I shout.

The man turns and looks at me with a smirk on his face.

"Don't grab my ass again!"

He continues to smirk. "Or what sweetheart?"

I wait for Jake to step in. To protect me, take care of me. He doesn't.

I smirk. "Or I'll file a lawsuit against you for sexual harassment."

I see the tiniest bit of fear at that possibility. I would never actually do it, but it was nice that he thought I could. I turn my attention back to Jake who is still standing at the table acting like nothing is going on.

"What was that?" I ask.

"Nothing," Jake says.

"Exactly. You didn't do anything after that man grabbed my ass!"

"What was I supposed to do? Go beat him up?"

"No. You were just supposed to stand up for me."

He sips on his beer slowly trying to keep his composure. He just doesn't realize that he is just giving me more time to get more fed up with him. I've had enough. He's not strong enough for me.

"I want to breakup."

I see the same anger in his eyes now.

"Karissa and I broke up almost two years ago now," Jake says.

I gasp. "So everything you told me was a lie?"

"No, everything was the truth, it just happened two years ago."

"Then why did you lie to me?"

"Because I knew if I let you back into my life you would hurt me again. And I was right. I was weak. I gave in to the temptation and then you fucked me over by fucking another man."

"I can't handle this right now. I just need you to go. We can talk later after this is all over."

I see the same pain in his eyes that I did when I broke up with him that night. But I didn't expect what he says next. I didn't expect that he could say anything that would hurt me so badly.

"It's not like you were the one who lost the baby, Scarlett. I know it's a painful time for your friends, but I can't just pretend like this didn't happen while you get over something that your friend is going through. I need to do this now."

When I look at Jake now, I see who he really is. He's not a nice man, like I thought he was. Because, the one time when he needs to be here for me, he isn't here. In fact, he's making it worse.

"Leave."

Jake narrows his eyes at me. "We're not finished yet."

"We are. Don't call me. Don't text me. I want your stuff out of my apartment by the time I get back there this evening. I don't want to see you again. As far as work goes, you can finish out your contract, but everything should go through Preston and not me. When your contract is over, I want you gone."

I turn around, and I walk back into Kinsley's room, leaving Jake. Forgotten.

And, as much as I thought I loved Jake before, I don't shed a tear when I leave him. Proving that I was wrong all along. I didn't love Jake. I'm not sure if I love any man.

The only thing I'm certain about is that I love Kinsley and her baby with Killian. And that's enough for now.

32

BEAST

Her text message plays over and over again in my head.

Me: Kinsley, my best friend, is in the hospital. I don't know what's wrong with her, but I'm afraid it's serious. I'm here, waiting.

I don't know what the message means. And I don't know why she sent it to me. I read the message over and over again, trying to figure it out. Trying to figure out why she sent it to me. Trying to figure out what she wants me to do.

I know it's a test. If I know her at all, I know that's what this is. A test.

I just don't know what she wants me to do. *Send her flowers? Text her something nice to make her feel better? Call her? Tell her I can fuck her to make her feel better? Or come to the damn hospital and reveal myself to her there?*

Despite telling her that I can reveal myself to her, it can't happen at the hospital. It can't happen anywhere in public. It has to happen on my terms.

But I need to do something for her. I want to do something for her. I want to do something to take away her pain.

Especially when I know I'm about to drop more pain on her.

So, I've typed out about a million different messages that I could send her. But each variation that I've tried hasn't seemed right. I've spent my entire day trying to figure out what to say.

That's when I realize there is nothing that I can say. Nothing that I say will make her feel any better. All she needs to know is that I'm here for her if she wants me to be. So, that's what I text.

Me: I'll do whatever you need. I'm here for you. If you need me.

I sent the message last night. It's now morning. And I still haven't gotten a response. I've tried to forget about it. I've tried to pretend her lack of response doesn't mean anything. That she's just mourning. That she's just in pain and trying to deal with it herself. And, even if I were there, there would be nothing I could do to help her. Not really.

But, still, her lack of response hurts. It makes me unsure if what I said was the right thing. It makes me unsure if she even still wants me in her life. I won't know until she texts me back. I can't do a damn thing but wait.

My phone buzzes on my coffee table. I jump up from my seat on the couch to get it. I cautiously stare at it until I see her name flash across the screen. I quickly open the message, needing to see what it says.

Beauty: Meet me at my apartment tonight.

She doesn't ask me if I can. She tells me. Tells me where and when to meet but not why or how to get there. She already knows that I know where her apartment is. Or at least she assumes, and she assumes right. I know everything there is to know about her.

And she knows the most important thing about me. She knows that I'll be there.

I knock on her door later that evening. I wait for what seems like an hour for her to answer. But it's in the same way that I answered her when she knocked on the hotel room door.

Beauty: Come in.

I grab the door handle, turn, and push the door open, unsure of what's going to be on the other side of the door. Unsure if this is the last time that she's going to care about me because, as soon as she sees me, she's going to hate me. I push inside the room, and to my surprise, it's completely dark. There isn't even any light coming in through the windows; they have been completely covered with window coverings.

"Beauty?" I call out.

I don't get an answer. I feel my phone buzz again in my hand. I open the message from her.

Beauty: Walk to the center of the room and find the blindfold. Then, put it on.

I read it slowly, over and over. She wants me to give up all my control. Just like I've made her do in the past. The only problem is, I have something to hide, and she doesn't. And, by me giving up my complete control, I'll have no control of when she decides to see who I really am.

I walk to the center of the room, which seems to be her

living room, and I find a blindfold lying on her coffee table. I pick it up, feeling the slick silk fabric in my hands. It'll do a decent job of keeping me in the dark although I'll probably still be able to see a sliver of light from the bottom. But it won't be enough to see her every movement. It won't be enough to tell if she decides to turn on the lights before I'm ready.

I tie the blindfold around my eyes, and then I wait. I wait for her to control me.

She makes me wait a long time. My anticipation and anxiety and need for her deepen with each second that passes. I need her. I need her right now. But she hasn't even made it clear if that's what I'm going to get. She might have already figured out who I am. She might be planning on killing me. She might be calling the police. She might be destroying my life. But I don't care. She's worth the risk if I get a chance of having her.

"I need you to make me feel good," she says suddenly.

When I hear her voice, I know she's standing in front of me. I suck in a breath and then let it out slowly. And then I smile because I know that she wants me to fuck her. I can hear it in her voice. That's what she needs. And I'm more than happy to deliver that to her.

"Gladly, Beauty."

I feel her hands on my face, running over my lips, and then they move down my body, feeling every inch of me over my clothes, studying my body with her hands. I don't know if she can see me or if she wants to see me. My guess is, she hasn't, or she would have already run from me.

She grabs my hand, moves me forward, and then lets go. "Undress."

It's one word. One simple word that says so much. It says, *I need you*. It says, *I control you*. It says, *I claim you*.

When she hears the last of my clothes hitting the floor, she says, "Take three steps forward."

I do and then stop. I wait.

"Kneel on the floor."

I do.

"Good boy," she says in the same way that I said, "Good girl," to her so many times before when she'd listened to my commands.

It feels strange, being on this side of things. Feels strange, giving up control. I never thought I would like it. But giving up control to her, I would gladly do it if it meant I got to have her.

I feel her hands touch my face again, followed by her lips. It's an intense feeling since I can't see her. I feel her long hair caressing my face as she kisses me. I reach my hand forward, needing to feel her. Needing to see if she's clothed or not. Needing to feel her body.

I reach out and find her face and immediately feel the fabric that is covering her own eyes. She blindfolded herself as well. She doesn't want to find out my identity tonight anymore then I want to show her.

She grabs my wrist as I reach out for her. "No more touching until I tell you to."

Her grip on my wrist is hard and firm, but I could still reach out and touch her if I really wanted to. I don't though. I listen to her and give her the control she needs.

"Good boy," she says again, her voice seductive, before her lips are on mine again.

Her hands are moving over my body, feeling me for the first time. And I catch my breath as she studies my body with her hands. First, my face that still has stubble from yesterday. Then, my chest. She feels over my heart that I know is beating rapidly. I know she can feel my anxiety and need growing for her. She moves her hand lower to my abs, counting each one with her fingers. Then, to my legs. She takes her time as she learns my every muscle. My every scar. The beat of my heart. When she has finally had her fill, she moves to my cock and roughly takes it in her hands. She studies it, too, even though she's had it inside her.

I let out a low growl when she touches me, needing her to know what she does to me with a simple touch.

Her hands move from my cock to my head. She grabs the sides of my head and pulls me forward. "Make me come with your tongue."

Her hands push my head onto her pussy. And I can't wait to devour her just like she asked. But I know I need to get her there slowly. I know I need to get her to feel every part of this. Forget the pain she's been dealing with for the last twenty-four hours.

I place my hands on her thighs, spreading her apart slowly and firmly in the chair she is now seated in. She lets me. I can feel her breathing. I can feel her pulse in her legs as I lower my head over her pussy. I breathe in and out slowly, letting my warm air move over her sensitive flesh. Trying to get her to focus on my breathing instead of what I'm afraid is still going through her head.

She's impatient though and can't wait for me. She grabs my hair on top of my head and forces my lips to touch her pussy. I can't help but grin at her being unable to control herself.

"Make me come. Now."

I slowly run my tongue around her lips, making circles around her clit. I feel her legs twitch in my grasp, and I know that I'm getting her excited. I continue to slowly run my tongue over her lips, then to her clit, and then back to her lips again—each time, spinning slightly longer and longer on her clit.

"Faster," she commands.

I move my tongue over her faster, and I am rewarded with a louder moan. I can't help myself. I need to feel more of her body, so I move my hands to her plump breasts. I feel her nipples harden. I move her nipples, rubbing them hard between my thumbs and first fingers, listening to more moans as I do.

I move my tongue faster and feel her legs tighten around my head.

Jesus.

I know she's close, but I want to make this last forever for her. I slightly slow my tongue, trying to make this last. Trying to give her as much time to enjoy this as humanly possible.

"Faster!" she screams.

I move faster as she commanded, and I feel her legs tightening on my head harder. I move my hands from her breasts to her legs, forcing her open for me. Forcing her to feel every drop of goodness that she can.

She screams, "Beast!"

It's a beautiful thing, feeling her come around my tongue, even though I can't see her. I can feel her, and that's almost as good.

Beauty doesn't wait until she's come down off her high. And she doesn't give me any warning. She stands quickly and grabs ahold of my body forcing me up. Her lips collide with mine, her hands go around my body, and I grab ahold of her, trying to figure out what she wants, but happy to give her whatever that is. She pushes me back, forcing me into a seat on the couch, and then she makes her intentions known as she mounts me.

"I need you. I need you to erase everything."

"I need you, too, Beauty."

She doesn't waste any time. She slides a condom over my cock, and then I'm inside her. Her hands on my shoulders, she's moving her body up and down over mine. I've never wanted anything more than to see through this blindfold, as I'm sure her breasts are bouncing up and down in front of my face. I want to see the pain disappear from her face. Still, her body moving over my cock is almost more than I can bear. Not being able to see just makes the sensation that much better.

I grab her ass and help her thrust on top of me.

We growl and pant and show how desperate we are for each other until we both come.

She doesn't stop there though. She hasn't had enough, and that's when I realize that the rest of my night is going to be spent here, fucking her. Trying to help her forget the pain.

We fuck on her kitchen table. On the stairs. In her bed. Over and over until she finally passes out in her bed.

When she finally passes out, I take the blindfold off and study her again for the first time today. She's beautiful as she sleeps. Even though I can still see the pain on her face. Even after all we've done all day, the pain is still there. All I did was push it from her mind for a few hours. But I can't think of a better way to spend my day.

33

BEAST

My phone buzzes, and I see that it's from my boss. I get up from her bed, leaving her to sleep. I don't answer right away. I'll call her back in a minute. I just need a second to gather my thoughts. To study her one last time while she's sleeping. Before she finds out the truth. Before she hates me.

I slowly get dressed as I watch her, secretly hoping that she'll wake up and discover who I am. Maybe if she wakes up before I fulfill my last job, she won't hate me.

She doesn't wake up, and I don't wake her.

I do walk over and kiss her one last time on her lips. Because, the next time I see her, I will tell her who I am. This might be the last time I get to kiss her, so I make it worth it.

Slowly, reluctantly, I turn and leave. I walk out of her bedroom and out of her apartment.

My phone buzzes again. My boss again. I don't answer again.

I will soon enough, but for now, I'm still trying to figure out what all my options are to get out of this mess. I'm afraid the only way I have a shot with her is by quitting. By getting out now before I do something that she won't forgive me for.

I continue out of her building. I can't though. If I don't finish the job, they will hunt us down and kill us both. I just have to finish the job and hope and pray that she forgives me.

My phone rings for a third time, and this time, I answer, "I'm on my way to the office now to tell you the plan."

34

SCARLETT

BEAST: *I want to tell you who I am. Just name the time and place. Or I'll come find you now and tell you. I can't wait much longer.*

Me: I have a fashion show to attend tomorrow night, followed by an after-party. You can tell me who you are before then, and then go with me as my date.

Beast: Fine. Just know that, after I tell you who I am, you won't want to take me as your date.

I stare at my phone, trying to understand his last sentence. I'm not sure why I wouldn't want to take him after he tells me who he is. But it's something I've been afraid of since the moment he wouldn't show me who he was. There's something wrong. Some reason that he won't just show me who he is.

I've formed hundreds of theories in my head. None of them make sense to me though. None of them have led me down the right track. The most likely scenario is that he is someone from my past, but I can't think of anyone who would fit his description. I can't think of anyone who speaks the way he does or controls me the way he does. I can't think of anyone.

It could be because he's hideous, and he thinks I'd run because of how he looks. But I've felt every inch of his body, and other than a few scars covering his torso, I didn't find anything hideous about him. And, even if he were, I'm not sure it would be enough to make me not want to be with him.

That leaves a third option. He's dangerous. He does something that I don't want to know about. He makes his money illegally. He does something immoral. Whatever it is, I'm sure it's not that bad. I'm sure it's something I can look past or that he could stop doing. It's not like we would need the money. I'm not looking for a man who brings in a lot of money. I'm just looking for a man who will love me and challenge me in the way that I need.

And I have a feeling that, after last night, Beast is that man. Last night was perfect. It showed me that Beast could give me what I needed, even at the cost of him giving up something he needed. And I know giving up control to me was not easy for him. Still, he did it anyway without question. He was the only one who was able to take me away from my pain, if only for a few hours.

The entire time I was with him, I wanted nothing more than to flick on the lights. I wanted nothing more than to open my eyes and see whom he was. I didn't though because last night wasn't about finding out who he was. Last night was about figuring out if he could give me what I needed when I needed it. And he did.

Tomorrow night will be about figuring out who he is and if I can live with whatever it is.

Today and tonight will be about Kinsley.

My driver, George, is driving me to her apartment. Killian needed to go into work for a couple of hours today, and I told him I would stay with her. I think the two of them, despite how much they love each other, need a couple of hours apart. They need a couple of hours to grieve on their own and not blame each other for what happened. A couple of hours not to feel the pain. Even as much as they try to help each other, it's hard because, anytime they look at one another, the pain is always there.

I just hope I'll be able to do something to at least distract her from her own pain.

George pulls up in front of her apartment building. He exits the car and runs around to open my door for me.

When he does, I step out. "Thank you, George," I say.

"It's my pleasure, Miss Bell. And I have to say, you have a hard job ahead of you. But, if anyone can do it, you can," he says.

I give him a tight smile but don't say anything. There are no words to say.

I walk into the building and onto the elevator, going up to the top floor. I'm somewhat surprised that they were still planning on living in an apartment when the baby came. I thought they would have wanted a house that they could turn into a home. I guess I don't know what their plans were for sure, but if I know Killian at all, I know it would have involved a surprise house that he'd bought for her at the last minute.

I swallow the lump in my throat. *How could their life be shattered in a single second? How could it shatter again after all the pain they'd endured? It's not fair. Not fair at all.*

When I reach Kinsley's apartment door, I use my key, not bothering to knock. I step inside. "Kinsley?"

I don't get an answer. I didn't think I would. When Killian left this morning, he said that Kinsley was still in bed and that he didn't want to disturb her. I'm guessing that's where she still is.

I turn right and walk down the hallway to their bedroom. I knock gently on the door. "Kinsley?"

I don't get an answer. I push the door open and see Kinsley sitting in a chair in the corner, staring out the window. She doesn't acknowledge that I'm here although I know she knows that I am here. There is no way she couldn't have heard me.

I try to figure out what I should do. I try to form some sort of plan. I have no idea what I should do. Should I take her out and go to the movies? Go to lunch? Go shopping? I don't think any of these things will make her feel better. But I have to try something.

I walk over to Kinsley and place my hand on her shoulder. "How about you go take a shower? Start there, and then we can figure out what we need to do after that."

Kinsley doesn't say anything. She just continues to stare outside.

I walk around and kneel in front of her. I shake her hands until she's looking at me. "Kinsley, go take a shower."

Kinsley finally sees me and nods. I help her stand and then wait in her bedroom until I see her walk into her bathroom. I hear the water running. I walk back into her living room, trying to figure out what I'm going to do, when I see the mess that is her apartment. Her kitchen is filled with dishes that need washing. Her living room is filled with clutter and clothes. Anything that's been brought into the apartment the last couple of days has just been dropped on the floor. Her bedroom wasn't much better. The bed was unmade, and there was plenty of dirty laundry on the floor.

I don't know what I'm going to do when Kinsley finishes getting ready. But I know what I can do right now. I'm going to clean.

I start picking up items off the floor in her living room. I pick up clothes and put them in her laundry room. Dishes go to the kitchen. And blankets get folded.

After I finish the living room, I head to the kitchen, lost in my own thoughts, forgetting entirely why I'm here, thinking I just need to clean. I turn on the warm water in the sink and begin washing the dishes by hand.

A few minutes later, I see Kinsley walk over and begin drying. Neither of us says anything to each other. We both just become lost in the task. We both just focus on cleaning, and that's when I realize that this is exactly what we need to be doing right now. Cleaning. Because, for whatever reason, cleaning is healing. It's calming and relaxing, and it's exactly what we both need.

We silently agree with one another that this is what we should be doing.

And, after an hour of silent cleaning, the silence turns into gentle talking. Not about anything of importance, just about simple things. The weather, the news, decorations that I like in her apartment.

We continue cleaning until we get to the bedroom door that I don't even think anything about. I just push it open, and a single tear falls from my eye when I see what's behind the door. It is Wesley's room. The room is not completely put together. The unfinished crib sits against one wall. The dressers are still in their boxes. Paint swatches, from grays to greens to yellows, cover the walls since they didn't decide on a color. There are baby clothes and supplies in the corner that still have tags on them.

Still, it is the baby's room, and I shouldn't have opened the door.

I turn around to see Kinsley and try to close the door quickly before she reacts. Before she loses all the progress she's made today.

"No. I need to go in there. I need to clean things up a little bit. I'm not going to get rid of things. We are going to have a baby at some point—whether that's through adoption, surrogacy, or me actually giving birth. It's going to happen. This just wasn't the right time. I need to be able to go into this room. Killian can't. It's too hard for him, but I need to be able to."

I nod and try to keep more of my tears back. Kinsley's going to be strong, so I can, too.

"Okay. But if you're not ready yet, it can wait. There's no rush on healing."

"I'm not rushing. I just...need this."

"Okay."

"Okay."

I hold the door open and watch Kinsley walk inside the room. She takes her time with running her hand over all the furniture. And then she walks over to the corner where the clothes and toys are. She picks up an item of clothing, holds it up, and cuddles it, breathing in the scent of baby that she'll never get to smell because the baby never got to wear it. Because Wesley never got to wear it.

When she removes the item from her face, I see her tears. And I lose it. I go over to her and hold her tightly, and we both cry. Somehow, these tears, so unlike the many tears before, are healing. I know that these tears are tears that we need to cry because, after they're gone, we'll feel a little better. We will be a little stronger. We will know that we can step inside this room and still survive.

"I think that's enough for today, don't you?" I ask.

Kinsley nods, and I lead her back out of the room. I don't really know what to do next, but we need to do something light after what we just went through.

"Want to watch cheesy romances with me?"

"Only if you order me Italian. Lots and lots of spaghetti and breadsticks."

"Deal."

I order her Italian for lunch, and then we both curl on a couch and begin watching cheesy romances for the next couple of hours. It doesn't even begin to take away the pain though. And I'm afraid the pain is always going to be there for both of us. And I wonder if I should have taken Kinsley out of this house, if that would've helped her heal more than just cleaning. Or, at the very least, it might've been more fun.

"Do you want to go with me to a fashion show tomorrow night?" I ask.

Kinsley thinks for a moment. "Are you sure you want to take me? I'm not sure I'll be a lot of fun."

I roll my eyes at her. "When are you ever not fun? Of course I want to take you." I already asked Beast to go with me, but if she says yes, finding out whom he is will just have to wait. My best friend is more important.

"Yes, I want to go," she says.

35

———

BEAST

I hate her message. I hate it. Because there can't be a next night after tomorrow night. Tomorrow night really is my only chance. After she texted me, I put the plan into place. My boss won't let me wait any longer. And I know, after I tell her who I am, she won't want to be with me anyway.

Tomorrow night is when I get my revenge.

Tomorrow night is when I destroy any chances of Scarlett and me ever being together.

Tomorrow night is when my life ends.

36

SCARLETT

"We look hot," I say, staring at Kinsley and myself in the mirror.

Kinsley had a hard time with finding a dress that she felt made her look sexy. It was especially hard since she's carrying a little extra weight from being pregnant. And that extra weight makes her think of Wesley. Thank God I was able to find a dress that showed off her curves. It's a black halter dress that hugs her curves and makes her look hot as hell.

I decide to wear a classic red dress, strapless and short.

"You look beautiful," Killian says as he walks into the bedroom. He goes over and gives Kinsley a hug.

She smiles at him as the two hug before he gives her a less than sweet kiss on the lips.

"I don't have to go. I can stay here with you, and we can have a nice dinner, followed by some other things," Kinsley says with a wink at Killian. "I'm sure Scarlett would rather take one of her boy toys anyway."

"First of all, I really don't want to hear that you two are planning on having sex tonight. Second of all, I don't have any boy toys, but if you don't want to come, that's perfectly fine," I say.

"No, it is not perfectly fine. Kinsley needs a night out, and I will be here, waiting to do some naughty things to you that involve chocolate and—" Killian says.

"Oh God! I'll be in the living room. I don't want to hear what you're gonna be doing afterward," I say, leaving the bedroom.

I look through my phone messages on the couch while I wait for Kinsley and Killian to most likely get in a quick fuck before we go. I sigh when I realize I still haven't gotten a response from Beast.

Is he upset that I'm not taking him tonight, like originally planned? Has he not gotten my message yet? Is he not sure if he's free tomorrow night?

I hate that I don't get to find out who he is tonight. But, if I'm honest with myself, I need a night out with my best friend, too. Because, if I were finding out whom Beast was tonight, I would be filled with anxiety. Anxiety does nothing to help healing. Tomorrow night though, I'll be ready. After a night of fun and relaxation, I'll be ready to face whatever he's going to tell me tomorrow.

"Ready," Kinsley says as she walks into the living room where I'm waiting for her.

I laugh when I see her. Her hair is a tangled mess, and she has red lipstick smeared on her cheek. But she looks happy, glowing for the first time in a while.

I get up off the couch and walk over to her. "You're almost ready," I say. I run my hand through her hair, smoothing the tangled mess. I wipe the lipstick off her cheek and then pull my lipstick out of my purse and reapply it onto her lips. "Now, you're ready. Let's go."

We arrive at the fashion event, and I can tell that Kinsley is excited to be back at an event like this. It's been a while since I have taken her to anything like this. Her smile is full on her face, and her cheeks are still flushed from whatever Killian did to her before.

We walk into the building and take our seats next to the runway. We have front-row seats even though this isn't one of my designers putting this on.

A few minutes later, the show starts, and models began stomping down the runway in various clothes.

"Oh my God, who would wear that?" Kinsley asks when one of the models walks onto the runway with her boobs practically falling out.

"I would! I think it's cute."

Kinsley laughs.

"Oh my God! Is that a penis?"

I turn to see what she's looking at when I see a male model walking down with what I'm pretty sure is his penis hanging out. I laugh. Designers will do the craziest things to get some press the next day.

"Yep," I say, covering Kinsley's eyes.

She laughs and moves my hand away from her face. I smile.

I made the right decision in bringing her here today. This is exactly what we both needed. A night of fun to be ourselves again. To rediscover who we are without men or babies or careers or anything else. Just as women.

The show ends, and we move to the after-party that is being held right next door. We are both immediately handed champagne as the party begins. I should be working tonight. Mingling with other designers and models and people in the business. Trying to spread my name and my brand. I don't though. I don't care about my business tonight. I just care about having fun with Kinsley.

"Let's go check out the appetizers. The shrimp looks delicious," I say.

Kinsley nods and follows. We walk over and pick up a skewer of shrimp that is delicious, followed by another plate of shrimp. Followed by tiny burgers. Followed by ham sandwiches. Followed by cheese fries. It's one of the strangest appetizers that I've seen at an event like this. But it's delicious nonetheless.

I feel my phone vibrate in my purse, and I reach into it, wondering if it's Killian trying to get me to take Kinsley home so that he can fuck her again. It's not.

Beast: You need to leave. It's not safe.

I stare at the message in confusion. *What does he mean, it's not safe? How would he know?*

Me: Why?

Beast: It doesn't matter. Just go. Now.

"I think we need to leave," I say to Kinsley.

Kinsley wrinkles her face at me. "Why? Is my husband trying to convince you that we need to go home? Because he can wait, you know," she says with a wink of her eye.

"No, it's not Killian. It's just—"

A familiar song comes on, and Kinsley grabs my hand. "We can go in a minute. I want to dance first."

I push away the strange feeling that we are in danger, and I follow Kinsley onto the dance floor. After two songs and a couple of shots, I forget all about Beast's messages. Kinsley and I are having fun, and that's what we need.

"I'm thirsty! Let's go get a drink," Kinsley says after a few more songs.

I nod and follow her off the dance floor. I pull out my phone again and this time it is from Killian.

Killian: I couldn't stay away. I'm on the West side of the building by the bathrooms. Don't tell her yet, but don't be surprised if she sneaks off to the bathroom and doesn't come back. It's just because I stole her.

I smile at Killian's text. We grab drinks, and then Kinsley decides she needs to use the restroom. My smile returns as I scan the crowd as we walk down a long hallway to where the restrooms are. As we walk, a man begins walking toward us and I'm sure it's Killian. The man is a tall, dark man. His hair is slightly messy on top of his head. His dark green eyes pierce my heart as he walks forward. Stubble covers his strong chin and neck. He's wearing a tuxedo that fits him perfectly, better than most men who are attending tonight. It's not Killian.

I can't stop looking at him as he walks toward us. I know this man. I've known this man for ten years. I've seen his picture on the news. I saw the police handcuff this man. I saw him go to jail for life for trafficking people, for killing people. For almost killing my best friend.

I watch this man pull a gun that seems to appear out of nowhere. I watch him aim the gun at Kinsley. I watch him fire before I have a chance to push Kinsley out of the way.

I don't know who screams. Me? Kinsley? An innocent bystander?

I have no idea.

He only fires one shot, and then he turns and walks in the other direction.

I turn to Kinsley. "Are you okay? Are you hurt?"

She grabs her chest and sinks to the floor. I'm afraid he shot her in the chest.

I search her body, but I find no blood. "Kinsley! Are you okay?"

"Yes, I'm okay. He didn't hit me. That was..." she says, breathing heavily.

"Yes, that was Nacio. The man who ran the trafficking ring with your family. The man who almost killed you." Silently to myself, I add, *the killer who is also my Beast.*

I think back to everything Kinsley has told me about Nacio. Everything that I have read in the newspaper about him and what happened to Kinsley. Everything that I've been told, or read, or experienced flashes through my head.

Nacio runs an organization along with Kinsley's Granddad. A terrible organization where they lie, smuggle, and kill for money.

Kinsley pretended to join the organization to try and stop them, but Nacio didn't believe she had the guts to lie, and smuggle, and kill. She needed to be tested.

Nacio shot a woman in cold blood.

Nacio tested Kinsley by telling her she must kill Killian.

...But then Nacio saved Kinsley by killing her Granddad when he tried to shoot her.

Is he really just a killer then?

And then there was that connection. When Nacio was arrested I saw him. Our eyes connected and I saw that there was more to him than just a killer. That he was a man that I felt an instant connection to.

I glance up and see Killian running toward us, anxious to see why his wife is lying on the floor. I don't know why I do it. It might be the worst decision I've ever made. But I need answers. I need to know why he decided to sleep with me. I need to know why he tried to kill Kinsley now when he'd saved her once before. I need to know why, despite being less than a couple of feet away when he shot her, he missed. Because it doesn't seem possible that he could miss. And, even if he did miss, he had plenty of time to get another couple of shots off before anyone could have stopped him.

"I'll be right back," I say to Kinsley. I begin running down the hallway after him as soon as Killian gets close enough to comfort Kinsley.

"Scarlett!" Kinsley shouts at me, trying to get me to stop.

But I don't stop, and I know the fear will keep her from coming after me.

I don't know where he went past the end of the hallway. I don't know where to go. I just run down the hallway and turn right when I reach the end, just like I saw him do. I know there's no way I can catch up to him. I'm in heels and a dress; he was in flat shoes. Even if I were in running shoes, I know I couldn't catch him.

My only chance is that he isn't running. My only chance is that he wants me to find him.

And I do.

I find him just as he is walking out the back of the building and into the darkness.

"Nacio!"

He stops when he hears me shout his name. He slowly turns and sees me. And I can see the pain on his face. Pain that I don't understand.

If anyone should be in pain, it should be me, not him. He's the one who deceived me. He's the one who fucked me even though he knew that, if I ever found out who he was, I'd hate him. He's the killer, not me. *Why the hell is he in pain when it should be me?*

When I see the look of pain on his face, every contradiction to who this man is comes to mind. He's a killer, yet he saved Kinsley almost ten years ago. And I'm pretty sure he just saved her now. He didn't kill her with a bullet even though he could have. And he'd tried to warn us to leave earlier.

He's a killer. Yet he's a man.

And, for some reason, I can't fucking understand why he is a man that I still want. He might not be a good man. He's definitely no knight in shining armor. But I want to give him a chance. I want to understand my beast and understand if he can give up killing.

I watch him study me, and I watch him understand the moment when I realize that I still want my chance with him. That I still want him. My beast. I have so many questions, and I don't even know where to start asking them.

I hear the sirens in the distance, and I know I don't have much time to ask my questions.

But, evidently, he has one of his own.

He holds out his hand to me and says, "Come with me?"

"Yes."

The End

Thank you for reading Definitely Yes! Want to read more of Scarlett & Beast's story? Find out what happens next here>>>Definitely No & Definitely Forever

FREE BOOKS

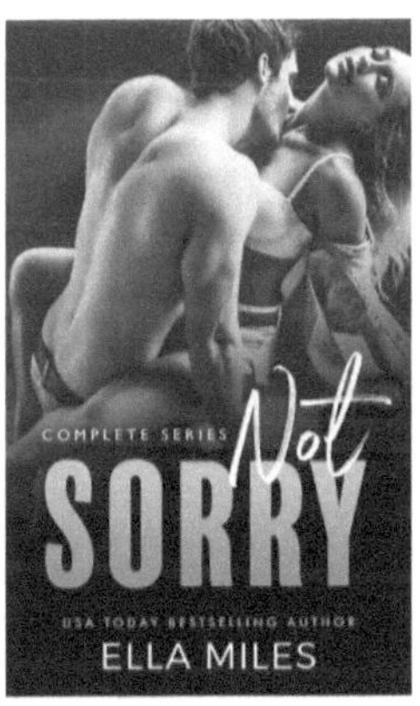

Read **Not Sorry** for **FREE!** And sign up to get my latest releases, updates, and more goodies here→EllaMiles.com/freebooks

Follow me on BookBub to get notified of my new releases and recommendations here→Follow on BookBub Here

Join Ella's Bellas FB group for giveaways and FUN→Join Ella's Bellas Here

Dirty Addiction

Dirty Revenge

ALIGNED SERIES:

Aligned: Volume 1 (Free Series Starter)

Aligned: Volume 2

Aligned: Volume 3

Aligned: Volume 4

Aligned: The Complete Series Boxset

UNFORGIVABLE SERIES:

Heart of a Thief

Heart of a Liar

Heart of a Prick

Unforgivable: The Complete Series Boxset

STANDALONES:

Pretend I'm Yours

Finding Perfect

Savage Love

Too Much

Not Sorry

ABOUT THE AUTHOR

Ella Miles writes steamy romance, including everything from dark suspense romance that will leave you on the edge of your seat to contemporary romance that will leave you laughing out loud or crying. Most importantly, she wants you to feel everything her characters feel as you read.

Ella is currently living her own happily ever after near the Rocky Mountains with her high school sweetheart husband. Her heart is also taken by her goofy five year old black lab who is scared of everything, including her own shadow.

Ella is a USA Today Bestselling Author & Top 50 Bestselling Author.

Stalk Ella at:
www.ellamiles.com
ella@ellamiles.com